GOOD GIRL

Copyright © 2022 by Ellie Sanders
All rights reserved.
No part of this book may be reproduced in any form or by any electronic or mechanical means, including information storage and retrieval systems, without written permission from the author, except for the use of brief quotations in a book review.

GOOD GIRL

ELLIE SANDERS

CONTENT WARNING

Just a heads up that is a hot, steamy, explicit story. It's dual POV so you get both the main characters emotions and understand their headspace.

BUT…. It's all about cheating. If you're not comfortable with this don't read it. It's as simple as that.

There is a taboo aspect in that it's stepdad and stepdaughter but they are both adults. The FMC is 21 so she's well over the age of consent (here in the U.K)

There's also some, albeit brief, instances of sexual assault but not by the male protagonist (obvs.)

There's lots of detailed, descriptive, extremely explicit scenes, including mild BDSM references (spanking), and oodles of daddy kink. It's a short, steamy, hot ride of a story that's for sure!

EDEN

One

The first time it happened was a mistake.

I thought the house was empty. I thought they were both out. It was early afternoon, mid-week, it wasn't an unreasonable assumption to make considering their work schedules.

I was watching porn. On the big screen. I mean if you're going to do it you might as well do it right, right?

It wasn't even that explicit, girl on girl, amateur, that's the stuff I prefer. Not the perfectly created videos. I like the bad camera angles, the way the women's bodies are more curvy, are more real. I'm not even bi I just get off on watching it. Call it a kink if you will. But I'm not ashamed. I like what I like.

And I'm sat, with a bullet vibrator, teasing myself, edging myself, making a mess that I know I'll have to clean up but I'm okay with that because right now I'm horny as hell and I need to play, I need an outlet, I need to cum.

And then I look up and Dominic is there. Stood in the doorway. Staring at me.

Fuck knows how long he's been there. Fuck knows who long he's been watching but he isn't taking his eyes off me.

I guess the sound of the women in the video got his attention. Maybe my moans did too because I wasn't quiet. The house was empty, there was no need to be.

But have I stopped? Have I covered myself?

No.

No I haven't. I'm just staring back with a tiny silver vibrator pushed against my clit, feeling it pulse, feeling my body flush as I get closer and closer and his eyes are dropping, taking in my pussy, taking in my splayed body, seeing as I'm working myself up to an orgasm right before his very eyes.

I should stop. I know I should. I have every intention of doing so but my legs are jerking, my body is shuddering and as he stands mute, I let myself topple over and give him the finale.

"Fuck." I hear him growl. I hear the lust in his voice too. He's not shocked. He's not angry.

He's turned on.

So I keep going, keep myself cuming, rolling the vibrator, circling it, making sure this orgasm lasts as long as it can under the watchful gaze of my stepdad.

"Eden." He says stepping forward and I pant out, letting him look where he likes. He's seen it all now anyway.

"Did you enjoy the show?" I ask.

He hesitates before nodding just a little and I lick my lips. My eyes are already taking in the bulge in his pants. Yeah he did enjoy it didn't he?

"Don't you want a taste?" I say. It's a risk. A big risk. A stupid risk and I know I shouldn't have said it but in my post cum haze I did.

He's hot. There's always been something about him that I've loved. I can't even articulate it but the way he is, the way he behaves, he makes me feel safe, makes me feel wanted when my own father abandoned me.

He shakes his head walking out but he's back barely seconds later, crossing the room, unzipping his trousers and getting his dick out.

My jaw drops. This man has been my father since I was thirteen. That's eight years. And now we're both crossing a line.

Only I started it.

I look up at him. He's still unsure. But his dick looks ready enough. Hell, I've never seen anything as inviting as his dick. He's a good eight inches, veiny, thick, circumcised too. If my limited experience is anything to go by this man's dick is a thing of beauty. Perfection itself.

I grin as I lean forward and swirl my tongue over the very tip.

"Eden." He groans.

"Yes Daddy?" I reply looking up at him and his eyebrows raise but I can see it, the word turns him on. I've never used the 'd word' before but he clearly likes that I've called him that in this moment. "Do you want me to suck you off?"

He grins. Taking my head in his hands and slowly he slides my mouth down over him.

Fuck I'm actually doing this.

I suck him slowly. If we're crossing this line I want to make the most of it, especially because this may be the one and only time. He groans as I work away, licking sucking, tasting him.

I fondle his balls. He's hairy but I don't mind it. It reminds me that this man is at least twice my age. A real man. A man of experience. Not just some little boy.

The sound of porno fills the air around us and if anything it heightens this, it makes it feel like we're in an orgy. It makes it feel like there's countless people in this room right now, all breaking rules, all being reckless, all fucking in some capacity or other.

"Can I cum in your mouth?" He asks.

I nod, pulling him out with a popping sound. "Yes please Daddy." I say and he groans before grabbing my head and forcing me back down on him.

Yeah he definitely likes me calling him that. And I like that he's taking control now.

I take hold of the base of him, pumping away just a little as I suck the top of him back in. I know I'm good at blowjobs. I've had enough practice because it's a neat distraction when a guy wants to fuck you but you don't want to fuck them. Sucking them off always solves the problem and besides, I enjoy the feel, the power of having a man's dick in my mouth and them literally melting with what I can do.

I let him slide down past my throat. I've gotten good a suppressing my gag reflex and I want Dominic to know and appreciate it in this moment.

"Ah fuck." He groans and I moan in response. I want him to know I'm enjoying this, that his dick is turning me on right now.

"We have to stop. Eden. Stop." He says gripping my head, pulling my hair, but I can feel already that he's too close. That he's going to cum and then his dick is jerking and he's pouring his hot salty juice all over my mouth as he growls out.

I pull away opening my mouth. I don't know why I do it but I want him to see, I want him to know how good he tastes. His cum drips down, trickling over my lips and he shakes his head shocked but clearly still turned on.

I swallow before blinking up at him.

"Eden."

"Did you not enjoy it?" I ask. He must have done. I could hear from his groans that he was.

He sighs, stepping back. "The fuck am I doing?" He murmurs running a hand over his face.

"Daddy?"

"Stop." He snaps. "Stop calling me that. This, this can't happen. This…" He points between us. "This can never happen. Terri can never find out about this."

Then he turns and storms out and I sit dumbfounded while the women on the porn video continue to moan and fuck.

DOMINIC

Two

The first time it happened was a mistake. I know it and she knows it.

I wasn't even meant to be back early but my meeting got cancelled and I decided to head back, have a little time to myself. Terri and I aren't exactly all that intimate anymore. She's gone off sex. She seems to only fuck on special occasions or when I pester her enough that she gives in.

And it's not exactly thrilling when we do fuck. A few thrusts, her lying there, staring up, probably imagining she's with someone other than me. To say the spark has gone is an understatement.

We practically live separate lives these days, what with my business and her new promotion keeping her away for weeks on ends so the sex is even rarer than before.

And it didn't help that I was on site all morning listening to my guys discussing their latest conquests in infinite detail.

I needed some stress relief and my balls needed a good empty.

So when I opened the door and hear her, her moans, her voice like a song, I was not only confused but curious. I've looked at her as my kid, my daughter, since I married her mother. I took her to after school classes, helped pick out her prom dress, played the protective dad not simply because I was married to her mother but because I care for her. I care for Eden.

And then she's there, legs wide open. Masturbating. I can see her cunt, even now I can see it. She's waxed, smooth. Perfect pink lips and a hole so small I know if I were to shove my cock in her she'd grip me so tightly.

Fuck, I'm doing it again.

It was a mistake. It won't happen again.

But the thought of her mouth on me, the feel of her hands as she fondled my balls. Jesus.

I'm hard. Right now, in this meeting when I need to be focusing on what is going on, I'm hard thinking of my stepdaughter and how I let her suck me off months ago, how I came in her mouth and how incredible she looked with my cum dripping down.

I wished I'd pulled her top off. Wish I'd seen her tits. Though I can imagine how good they look, I wish I'd felt them, felt her nipples harden for me. For her Daddy. My Eden. My very own slice of Paradise.

Fuck I need to not think that. Not again. She can't call me that. I can't call her that. She's my stepdaughter for fucksake and if Terri ever finds out she'll be devastated.

And I'll be ruined.

One of the investors asks a question. Something about the latest liabilities on our balance sheet. Timothy my Finance Director answers before I can and thank god he does because all I can think of is how my stepdaughter would feel as I fucked her.

I'm a monster I realise. I'm a pervert. There's something very wrong with me to even think of Eden like that.

And anyway it's been months. Absolute months. I've been avoiding her since. Working more, making sure to not be in the parts of the house she likes to frequent.

"Well I think that's about everything." Timothy says and I nod. Pretending that I've been paying attention.

"Great job." The investors say. But of course they think that, I've given them year on year growth, above market growth at that. My construction company is the best in the city, the best in the area. We've won national awards for our work and our charitable arm has made everyone in the room look good. What's not to be happy about?

"See you at the gala." Marcus their head honcho says and I smile. Our annual gala is a thing of legends. It was Terri's idea, years ago, when she showed an interest in what I did, when our relationship was fresh, new, admittedly when we both worked at it.

And the gala is a way we can show off our philanthropy. Raise money. Give back too. We've got a whole range of projects going from helping homelessness to getting kids of the streets. Of course Terri thinks it's all a waste now but I disagree. I was a street kid. I knew what it was to go hungry, to fight for every scrap and just because I've made it now, just because I'm rich doesn't mean I'll turn my back on where I came from.

"Drinks?" Tim says.

"Yeah. I could do with one." I say. It's been a long week. And with Terri away with work I don't want to go home right now and risk being caught with Eden because I don't know what she would do.

And more than that I don't know what I would do.

EDEN

Three

Thank fuck it's Friday. That's all I can say. I've had a bitch of a week. My assignment came back with a shit grade, despite me sweating actual blood on it and my boss put me down for all the night shifts he could get away with so my body clock is all messed up, making me even more cranky.

The only good news was my mum's been away on a business trip so I've managed to avoid her going off about the state of my room, and the fact I've loaded the fridge with more junk food than ever.

I'm not even that big a drinker, I don't really like alcohol but tonight, tonight I just need a drink and some time off.

"Eden, over here." Katie my best friend calls as I walk into the new swanky bar they've decided we have to check out this evening. We're only just old enough to be allowed in here, but the fact we both look mid-twenties means no one has challenged us.

And the fact we're both wearing short, slutty dresses definitely helps.

"How long have you been here?" I ask eyeing up the half-drunk cocktail.

"Not long. Max picked me up straight from work." She says sipping her drink. "Aron is here…" She adds smirking.

"Where?" I ask glancing around. It's not that I don't want to bump into him it's just I'm tired and I wanted a girls night, not a night of pandering to his ego.

"Over by the bar." She says jerking her head in the direction of where he's stood staring at me.

"Fucksake." I mutter.

"What's the matter? I thought you two were good?" She says.

"Yeah, we are." I reply. Though it's not exactly true. All we do is argue these days. Bicker. And tonight I just can't be bothered with it. "Want a drink?"

"I'm good." She says as Max turns up draping his arm around her shoulders.

"Aron's looking for you." He says.

"Yeah I heard." I reply before wandering off because if I don't make an effort it'll only piss him off more.

"Baby." He says as I lean on the bar. Even his voice is annoying me. And to call me baby? Jesus could he be any more cliché?

"I've had a long week." I murmur.

"Is that why you've been ignoring my messages?" He says narrowing his eyes.

"I've been busy. I've had college and I got put on nightshifts."

He snorts. "You don't need to work Eden. I don't even know why you bother."

I grit my teeth and turn around trying to get the bar man's attention because right now I need a drink or I'll punch his god damn face in.

It's true I don't need to work. Dominic gives me an allowance. A more than generous allowance. He also pays all my college tuition despite my mother earning enough money to do it herself. Only she won't.

Perhaps that's why I insist on having a job, on paying my own way where I can. I don't want to be like her, acting like a gold digger, and all the allowance Dominic gives me I intend to pay back.

Of course my mother scoffs at me when I state that. As if I'm a silly little girl who has no idea what the world is like. She then tells me that I'll never do it, I'll never manage it. That I'll end up like her dependent on a man and she'll be there saying 'I told you so'.

She's half the reason I'm still in this city, because she wouldn't let me go to college anywhere else. She said it was because of the expense, like she didn't want Dominic wasting any more money on me, but we both know it's about control. She wants me here, where she can keep her eye on me but not in a motherly, protective way like other parents would. Not my mother.

"Vodka coke." I say to the bar man. "No ice."

"Got ID?" He asks and I huff as Aron laughs.

"She's twenty one mate." He says.

"Sure she is." The barman replies. "So she won't have a problem proving it."

"I forgot it. Left it in my car." I say and he rolls his eyes. It's not actually a lie. It is in my car because I got pulled over the other day and dropped it behind one of the seats.

"Sure you did love. You planning on driving home after, adding DUI to your list of crimes?"

I cross my arms. "Fucksake."

"Tell you what, I'll give you a coke, no vodka, no ice." He says. "And I'll let it pass that you're too young to even be in this place."

"What a gentleman." I snap and he laughs grabbing a glass and filling it up.

"You're welcome." He says. "That'll be £2."

"Put it on my tab." Aron says.

"Fuck off I can pay myself." I state pulling out a £5 note and passing it quickly over.

The bar man looks between us and, as Aron walks off annoyed, he takes the money.

"I want the change." I say. No way is he getting a tip right now.

"Eden."

My stomach drops as I hear his voice and I turn almost reluctantly to look at him. He does a slow take of me, from my heels, up my legs, to my tight bodycon dress, and he stops when he reaches my face.

I gulp. Of all the bars he had to be in he just had to be in this one, tonight.

He's wearing a shirt. It's open slightly and I can see the hint of chest hair. Despite the scowl on his face, despite the irritation, he looks fucking hot right now.

"Why are you here?" He asks.

"I'm just out with a few friends." I reply. "I'm not even drinking."

"Not for want of trying." The barman says placing my change on the counter with his impeccable timing.

I turn to curse him and Dominic grabs my arm. "How much have you drunk?" He asks.

"I haven't." I say. "And besides I'm an adult, I can have a drink if I want too." I half snap.

He opens his mouth to reply but I don't wait to hear it. I pull my arm free and walk away. It's the first time he's touched me, been around me, hell even properly spoken to me in months and this is how he wants to be? And anyway I'm perfectly entitled to be here, just as he is.

My skin is tingling where his grip was. My body is flushing with something stupid. And all I can think about is how his face looked when I slipped his dick in my mouth.

"Isn't that your stepdad?" Katie says as I join them. They're sat around, all my friends are here now, a big group of us. Aron is still shooting me daggers but I ignore it sipping my coke.

"Yeah." I murmur.

"And he's drinking here too?" She says.

"Looks like it." I reply glancing back, stupidly, and making eye contact with him again. He's with Timothy his Finance Director and as I stare Eric, his brother, walks in. Just fucking fantastic.

There's a bunch of women hanging around them now, congregating. Eric and Dominic are a big enough name in this city to get attention wherever they go and I feel a streak of something akin to jealousy as I watch them try to flirt with the man I know I shouldn't want.

DOMINIC

Four

"**W**hat's gotten into you?" Eric asks as I glare into my beer glass.

"Does something have to be up?" I reply.

He lets out a laugh like he knows me better than I know myself. Like the fact that we're brothers gives him the ability to read me better than anyone else.

"You were fine till you walked in here." Tim says. There's a woman hanging off his arm but he's already ignoring her, his eyes fixed to his phone while he plays some slots game.

And then he spots her. But of course he fucking does.

"Jesus, is that Eden?" He says.

I nod. Not looking. Because I know, if I do, I won't look away. That dress she's in is far too mature, far too revealing. I doubt any full bloodied man in this place hasn't stared at her, hasn't imagined fucking her by now.

I clench my fists. It shouldn't matter, I tell myself. It doesn't matter. The girl can wear what she wants. Do what she wants. She's an adult. She's entitled to have a little down time every now and then. It doesn't matter that she's even in this bar. She's not my kid anyway. Not really.

"Should she be here?" Eric asks. His daughter, my niece, has just gone to med school and the tales he tells of what she gets up to. He gets it. I know he gets it.

"She's an adult." I state. "She's of age."

"Fucking hell mate, how do you live with that?" Timothy groans.

"What?" I snap.

Eric narrows his eyes half glaring at Tim. "The fuck?" He mutters.

"Look at her." Tim says and I do, against my better judgement I turn my head and I know I'm staring, lusting after her too.

She's dancing. The whole group of them are. The dancefloor is packed, heaving, everyone is enjoying their Friday night but the only person I see is Eden, and fuck me the way she moves her body. The way her ass looks as she rolls her hips.

"The fuck are you doing?" I growl at Timothy. He's been staring too. Staring at my stepdaughter.

"Sorry mate but if she dresses like that what do you expect?"

"She's twenty one." I growl.

"She's legal." Tim jokes and I swear I might just hit him.

"She's his stepdaughter." Eric says as I slam my fist onto the counter. Shame I couldn't remember that two months ago when I was eagerly getting my cock out for her.

"Yeah and where's your wife right now?" Tim asks. "Because that's her kid there and I see you doing more for her than that woman ever does."

"Leave it alone." I mutter. He's always making comments about Terri. About how she isn't much of a wife, about how she's only after my money and though a part of me wonders if he might be right, I still married her, I still care for her on some level, and besides it's not just her, Eden is part of the package, and I won't let her down.

I glance back, stealing another look at her. She's with that useless flop of a boy she's been dating. They're arguing. Obviously arguing. I smirk because it makes me happy to see her putting him in his place. He grabs her, grabs her ass and she slaps him, pulling away.

I go to get up, to intervene, but Eric's already seen me move and he's holding me back.

"Not your place." He mutters.

And then she's storming off, grabbing her bag, leaving the bar with her friend Katie hot on her tails.

"See?" Eric says. "She's probably already heading back home for a cup of hot milk and bed."

I roll my eyes. I doubt Eden's doing that but right now I have to let it go because I'm acting suspiciously.

"Where is Terri anyway?" Tim asks as I down my beer and order us all another.

"Brussels. She's got some big project she's delivering." I state. I should be more proud of her really. She's a successful woman, she's got a good job, she works hard.

He snorts like he doesn't believe it. Like she's lying or something but that's Timothy. I don't know why he hates Terri so much but he does. He acts like she's a gold digger, but she was the one who chose to go back to work, even when I offered to give her enough money to stay at home. She insisted. And she puts in the hours, puts in the overtime. My wife works hard.

And that thought makes me feel even more guilty. About what I did. About what an absolute jerk I was. She didn't deserve it. She didn't deserve to be betrayed like that. And Eden? She didn't deserve it either, no matter how into it she was at the time.

It was my fuck up. My mistake.

I know it. I'm owning it, at least to myself.

And yet even now, even in this moment, I can't get the thought of Eden's needy cunt out of my head.

EDEN

Five

I storm out of the bar. Thankfully Katie comes with me though I half expected her to stay with her boyfriend. I certainly wouldn't have minded if she had.

She races to catch up just as I try to hail a cab.

"What's wrong?" She asks.

"Aron." I mutter. "He's such a prick."

She rolls her eyes. I know she thinks I'm being a drama queen but I'm so sick of Aron treating me like shit. Treating me like I'm just here for his amusement. That I should be honoured by his attention, flattered that he'd even consider glancing my way.

"What's he done now?" She says.

"He just won't stop pushing me." I say.

"About what?"

"Sex."

She smirks. "What's the big deal?"

I bite my tongue. Everyone thinks I've done it. Everyone in our group has. I'm the only virgin. Not that it's that big a deal really, it's just, I don't want to sleep with Aron. In truth, I don't even want to be with him. I only hooked up with him because he's been chasing me for ages and I needed a distraction, I needed something to take my mind off of Dominic.

I need to prove to myself that there were other men. Only look how that turned out.

"I'm not ready to sleep with him yet." I say.

"You've been together for almost two months." She states like there's a set timeframe for all of this.

"Yeah that doesn't change how I feel." I reply. I've been pushed already into doing more than I want with him, in giving away pieces of myself, albeit reluctantly, to a man who's used to getting his own way because of who his family is and I'm done with giving anymore.

A taxi pulls up and I open the door. "Are you coming?" I say.

She sighs before following me in. "Where?"

"My place. I've had enough of bars for one night." I reply.

"Fine but there better be alcohol." She says.

I laugh. My mother has a whole stash, she won't notice if a few bottles go missing. And besides what will Dominic do if he catches me actually drinking? Maybe he'll spank me as punishment?

I shake my head slightly, trying to erase the thoughts. God I need to sort myself out. It was a mistake. A big mistake. One, that Dominic has made more than clear, won't be repeated again, and the more I cling to this, the more I think about my stepdad and his glorious dick the more I'm digging a hole for myself.

"What are you grinning about?" Katie asks as she stares at me.

"Nothing." I say.

But it's not true.

I'm thinking about him. Even now. Even when I'm telling myself not too. My mother has been gone for two weeks and I know he's been making himself scarce, avoiding me, like he's scared I might pounce on him at any opportunity. If I was in bed right now I'd be making myself cum to that idea, to the notion of Dominic, being chased by his wanton stepdaughter.

Fuck I'm ridiculous, I think, as we speed through the city to my stepdad's mansion where I'd dearly love him to touch me. Where I'd dearly love to touch him again.

DOMINIC

Six

The lights are all on when I get back. It's early morning. She should be in bed and yet it's more than abundantly clear that she isn't.

I guess I should be grateful that she's here. That she's safe. That her douche of a boyfriend hasn't done anything to harm her and yet all I feel is annoyed.

Timothy is smirking like he knows somethings up. Like he's expecting my stepdaughter to be exhibiting herself again.

I unlock the door and the music is blaring. We walk through and her friend is dancing on the god damn coffee table as she laughs and swigs from an actual bottle of wine.

"The fuck is this?" I snarl turning the music off and the sudden silence is deafening.

Eden gulps, her face falling as she looks at me.

"Get down now." I say to Kate or whatever her name is. She half stumbles, falling onto the couch and the way her legs are splayed would give me a birds eye view up her dress though I keep my eyes fixed on Eden.

Her friend hiccups before belching and Eden gasps.

"Jesus Katie." She murmurs as if that's the most outrageous thing they've done all night.

"You need to go home." I say to the blonde.

"No, she can't go in that state." Eden replies scowling at me.

"And who's fault is that?" Timothy says.

She glares at him too. "We were just letting off some steam." She mutters dropping her eyes, looking like she's actually ashamed of her behaviour. I don't even know why I'm so annoyed, it's not like it's that big of a deal really and I know I'm overreacting. This is her house, she should be able to bring friends back if she wants, hell she's a student. That's what students do.

"Fine. She can sleep here. But you're done drinking." I say grabbing the bottle from her hand and she nods.

"I'm sorry." She says so quietly I barely hear her.

She helps her friend up and we hear them stumble through the house to Eden's room.

"I think she enjoys keeping you busy." Timothy says. "I think she enjoys being a handful."

I shake my head. She's not. Not really. Eden isn't normally like this. She's a good kid. She works hard. In fact, I've never seen her drunk before. Seen her like this before.

Maybe it's me that's made her act out. Maybe I caused this. I run my hand over my face. Timothy called her a handful and by god would I love to get a handful.

"Drink?" He says.

"Yeah." I reply.

He comes back with a beer, top already off, and I sip it while he puts a war movie on. I'm not even watching it, I don't even like war movies, not really, but when he suggested heading back I figured it was a good way to ensure I didn't do anything stupid. Anything reckless.

But barely a few minutes in I see her, walking down, sitting on the couch opposite us. She's wearing a skimpy pair of shorts and a t-shirt. Normally I'd never notice them. Normally I wouldn't stare but normally a stepdad doesn't fantasise about face fucking his stepdaughter while his best mate is sat beside him.

"Why aren't you in bed?" I ask her.

She shrugs. "I can't sleep. I've been working night shifts. My body clock is all messed up."

I grunt in reply. I guess it makes sense, though why she has to sit down here with us I don't know.

She shifts, putting her legs out on the pouf, stretching them. I don't think she's even meaning to be provocative but even Timothy stares and I give him a pointed look.

He downs his beer and gets up. "Want another?" He asks.

"Sure." I reply. I'll take anything to distract me from Eden right now.

"Eden?" He asks.

"No." I say before she can reply and she smirks just a little but says no thank you so demurely I feel my cock awaken.

He shrugs before heading to the kitchen and we sit awkwardly staring at each other while the film flickers on.

"What's going on?" I ask her.

She shakes her head. "Nothing."

"Eden, I know something's up. This isn't you. You're not reckless. You're not stupid."

"No?" She says leaning forward, crossing her arms under her tits and I can't help but drop my eyes to them for a moment. "What about what we did? Wasn't that reckless?"

I shake my head. Let out a snarl under my breath. I'm so aware that Timothy is going to walk back in at any moment.

"You need to forget it. Pretend nothing happened." I state.

"Is that what you've done? Forgotten it? Forgotten me?" She says as we hear footsteps.

I want to reply. I want to tell her that of course I haven't. That I spend every god damn waking hour thinking of her, thinking of how I can be with her, and when I see her I spend every second devouring her skin, imagining that she's wrapped around me, imagining that I'm sinking my cock into her tight little cunt as she begs me for it and all the while I make sure I'm not alone with her because if I am, I know I won't be able to control myself.

Timothy walks in, placing the bottles on the table.

"I got some popcorn for you." He says passing the bowl to Eden who smiles and thanks him.

And as he sits down I can't help watching, envying, as she puts one cornel after another into her mouth, seeing as she parts her lips, seeing as the sugar sticks to them the way my cum did.

GOOD GIRL

I shift, adjusting my trousers through the pocket as best I can, my cock is so hard right now and as my eyes flicker back to her I see she's seen it. That she knows.

EDEN

Seven

I'm avoiding him. It's ironic really. First he was avoiding me and now I'm avoiding him.

I just don't know how to deal with this. Maybe I'm not mature enough. Maybe I'm not experienced enough but when my mum returns I'm actually grateful for her presence for once.

We go out for dinner. She makes a big fuss about wanting some quality family time, though she spends the entirety of her time checking her phone as if we're not even there.

She chooses a fancy restaurant. We all have to dress up and no doubt she'll make Dominic pay. Not that he'll mind. He's too kind, too caring to mind.

I've put on a polka dot wrap around dress. It stops perfectly between the top of my thighs and my knees. But my mother is still giving me shitty looks as if I've worn something outrageous. My hair is down, falling in dark thick curls and I know I look good, in a presentable yet still attractive way.

Dominic's wearing a navy silk shirt. With black pants, and a Hermes belt that catches the light as he moves. His hair looks like he's been running his fingers through it with just a few silver streaks highlighting his age. In this moment it's making him look like a silver fox.

I bite my lip, trying not to stare because I shouldn't even be lusting after a man so much older than me, let alone what we are to one another.

My mother's wearing a tight fitted, dress that clings to her body showing off her curves. Showing off how attractive she is. And she is. Even someone half her age would be proud to look like she does. Besides it's not like she's had surgery to keep her figure, she works out a lot, she should be proud.

Dominic places his hand on the small of her back, guiding her as they walk in front and it's hard not to feel a stab of jealousy. She doesn't seem to notice though, she doesn't even react as he touches her. It's as if she doesn't care for his affection but I wonder if that's just the bitterness in me that thinks that.

We sit down, Dominic opposite me and my mother between us. I keep my eyes on my menu, my eyes on my plate. I can't look at him though I feel his glances every so often.

When we're done ordering my mother makes a point of asking about my college work.

I tell her about my latest assignment, about the new project I'm on. About the fact that I'm being put forward for a national prize for my last dissertation. She scoffs. She belittles and Dominic frowns, taking her hand, and then he tells me what a great achievement it is. He tells me how proud I should be, and that I deserve a prize for how hard I'm working.

"She doesn't work hard." My mum says cutting across him.

"That's not true Terri. She's worked non-stop these last few weeks." He says like he hasn't been hiding out, pretending I don't exist.

My mother throws me a look. "No harder than anyone else though."

I roll my eyes and take a sip of my drink. I know why she is how she is. She sees my dad in me. When she looks at me that's all she sees, her own failures, her own mistakes. It doesn't help that I have his olive skin tone, his dark hair, his looks. If I were blonde, if I were pale, if I resembled her more then perhaps she'd care more.

Dominic gets up to use the toilet and my mother calls the waiter for another bottle of white. She's drunk most of the first by herself though she's good at handling her drink even I can tell she's getting drunk now.

"Don't think I don't know what you're doing." She says.

"With what?" I say.

"With my husband." She states.

I gulp. There's no way she knows. No fucking way.

"I know you're turning him against me. I'm not an idiot. I can see the games you're playing. You're just like your father. Manipulative."

I shake my head. It's not like I have been intentionally manipulating him. But I did cross the line. Even I know that. I guess I deserve her derision right now.

Dominic comes back and he looks between us. "What have you two been discussing in my absence?" He says smiling.

"Just about her college." My mother says. "Eden is thinking of transferring."

My eyes flit to her as she speaks. What the hell is she saying right now?

"Transferring where?" Dominic asks.

"Edinburgh." She says before taking a sip of her wine.

The fuck? That's hundreds of miles away. Hell, that's the other side of the country. She says I'm manipulative? She's trying to send me away after forcing me to stay in the first place. And anyway, I'm in my final year, I can't transfer now without having to retake.

Dominic frowns looking at me. "Is that true?" He says.

I open my mouth to speak but my mother waves across me. "Of course it is. She wants some independence Dom, she's a big girl. Let her spread her wings. Grow up a bit."

I shake my head slightly. There's nothing I can do in this moment and I won't pick a fight. But my heart sinks anyway because it's more proof of the fact my mother doesn't really love me. That she doesn't really want me. That I'm a burden to her. That I always have been.

"Excuse me." I say quietly getting up. I need to get some fresh air. I need to get some space. I need to get myself together before I end up crying.

I stand outside, letting the cool evening breeze hit me. I don't want to leave and I sure as hell won't let her bully me out. Perhaps I can speak to Dominic separately, plead my case. Perhaps he might listen. Though I feel like he won't. I've messed it up. I've messed everything up.

"Eden?" A woman says. "I thought that was you."

I stifle the groan as I see Aron's mum making her way towards me with her husband and my dick of a boyfriend in tow. But of course he would be here right now.

"Hi." I say smiling.

"We didn't realise you were here." His dad says as if this is a big public outing.

"We're just grabbing some dinner." I say.

Aron is giving me a look. We haven't spoken since I stormed off. Though he's hounded my phone with messages.

"Well we'll see you inside." His mum says looking between us. "It's good to see you Eden."

His dad nods before they walk in.

"Why aren't you replying?" Aron says as soon as they're out of earshot.

"Because you pissed me off." I state.

He snarls. "So you're just ignoring me then is that it?"

"I'm not ignoring you. I'm just not talking to you, until I cool off enough." I state.

He scoffs. "You're such a drama queen."

"And you're such a dick." I snap.

He grabs my arm, wrenching me round and slamming my back into the wall. "I don't like being spoken to like that." He says.

"And I don't like seeing my stepdaughter being manhandled like that." Dominic growls from what feels like out of nowhere.

Aron narrows his eyes. "I'm not hurting her."

"I don't give a fuck. Remove your hand before I do."

He makes a big play of letting go of me. "Calm down dude, she's my girlfriend."

Dominic's eyes flash at the word. "Why don't you run along and find your parents? No doubt they're looking for you."

Aron smirks before grabbing me and kissing me as if I'd want him to right now.

"Fuck off." I hiss as he laughs and walks into the restaurant.

"Eden." Dominic says as soon as he's gone. "What the hell do you see in that boy?"

I shrug. If I'm honest I'm done with him. I have been for a while but I won't admit that right now.

"He's got money." He continues. "He's got connections sure, but I'd thought you'd aspire to more things than just material gains."

I scowl. "You really want to have this conversation right now?"

He frowns and I shake my head.

"Why don't you just ship me off to Edinburgh? Then you won't have to think about me anymore." I state going to walk inside only he grabs me. Not as hard, not nearly as aggressively as Aron did.

"You don't want to go, do you?" He says.

"Why would I?" I snap back.

He runs his eyes over me, as if he's trying to read me. "It might be for the best." He murmurs.

"Maybe for you." I reply pulling myself free heading back inside before I say something I'll regret.

DOMINIC

Eight

It feels like we spend the rest of the meal in silence. At least me and Eden are because Terri is talking away, telling stories about her work. I listen as much as I can, make a few comments here and there but my attention is on her.

On Eden.

She's not looking at me. She won't look at me even once.

I know I shouldn't have said it. I know I should have kept my opinions to myself but it does make sense. It makes a lot of sense. Besides if she goes, then perhaps this incessant want for her might go too.

I can see her arm's already bruising. I can see where that boy's fingers pressed into her skin and I feel a flash of anger that he had the nerve to do that. If his dad wasn't who he was I'd drag the piece of shit out right now and beat him to a pulp.

When the meal's done I pay the bill and we get a taxi home. I wasn't planning on drinking but being sat there with Eden in front of me and her mother beside me I needed something to steady my nerves. Besides Terri drinks enough to not make any comments.

Terri gets in the front and I sit in the back beside her daughter. My stepdaughter.

She stares out the window. Tilting her body so that her back is angled towards me.

I can still make out the bruise.

"Has he done that before?" I ask quietly.

"Done what?" She says glancing back.

"Grabbed you, hurt you?"

She narrows her eyes. "What do you care?" She half whispers. She's so angry right now and I don't even understand where it's all coming from.

"I care Eden."

"Then why are you sending me away?"

"I'm not." I reply glancing to where her mother is sat, only she's drunk so much she's half dozing and is blissfully unaware of this conversation.

"Yes you are. You said it would be for the best."

"Eden. I have to protect you."

"Is that what you were doing before?" She asks. "Protecting me?"

"Fuck." I growl and I feel the taxi driver glance to look at me in the rear-view mirror.

I shake my head, hold my tongue. I can't say anything more right now even if I wanted to because we've got another person hearing all of this and I'm a big enough player in this city for any indiscretion to be front page news.

We pull up by the house. Terri wakes up as we come to a stop and I help her get inside. I don't look back at Eden but I know she's behind us, walking slowly, as if she's on her way to her own execution.

I half carry my wife in, cursing her drinking habits and making a note of raising it with her again. When she's undressed, when she's in bed, I leave her to it. She can sleep it off, snore it off while I sleep in the spare room.

I head to the kitchen for a nightcap.

"If he'd hit me, if he'd really hurt me would you have done something?" Eden asks and I jump because I didn't realise she was there. Sat in the darkness. Brooding.

"Of course I would." I say. "And he did hurt you. You've got bruises."

She shakes her head. "You're full of shit."

"Excuse me?"

"You are. You act like you have my best interests at heart but you don't give a fuck what I want." She snaps back slamming her fists into my chest before I can stop her.

"Eden." I growl, grabbing her hands.

"Don't touch me." She says pulling away. "Don't you dare fucking touch me."

"What do you want from me?" I ask and she stumbles back slightly, as if she's drunk too, only she's not had a drop of alcohol.

"You know what I want." She half whispers before leaving the room. Running to her own.

And as I watch her shadow disappear, I so desperately want to follow her.

EDEN

Nine

We're having a pool party. A family get together plus extras. My mother's invited friends from work, her boss and some other colleagues too. Dominic of course has Eric and Timothy here.

I asked Katie but she's busy with some family thing too. So it's just me, and my entire family who look on me like the black sheep, like the millstone around my mother's neck. Like I'm responsible for my father walking out on us when I was a baby.

Sins of the father and all that I guess.

Only she hasn't done that badly despite my existence. Dominic has given her a life she'd never have dreamed of. Never have had, had my father stuck around. But that fact is conveniently ignored.

I've spent most of the afternoon chatting to aunts and uncles. Various relatives. They all seem to ask the same thing, how's college, how's my job, have I got a boyfriend and what do I want to do when I've finished my degree. As if my life is on some conveyor belt of monotony.

When I finally escape them it feels like a small mercy.

My younger cousins are screaming, running around the garden, generally being obnoxious. I shake my head grabbing a drink and go seek the solitude of the hot tub.

Thankfully no one else is in here and it's nicely tucked away so I don't have to make polite conversation about my job, or my course, or life, or anything really. I can just have some space, some thinking time too.

I toss my dress off, sink into the warmth and sit until my skin goes wrinkly. Until I've drunk all my coke and finished lamenting the fact I couldn't think of a decent enough excuse to get out of this whole damn day.

I know if I get out I'll only have to face them and it's easier to stay here, play the antisocial teenager if you will, hiding. I lay back shutting my eyes, pretending I'm anywhere other than where I am.

Only someone gets in.

I grit my teeth deciding not to look at them, not to acknowledge them. But they sit beside me. Right beside me, as if this tub isn't big enough for eight people.

And then their hand sneaks up my leg. I pause, half thinking I'm imagining it because who the fuck would be touching me right now? But as their fingers move to between my thighs I jolt up.

"What the fuck?" I say.

"Ssssh." Timothy says grinning.

"What the fuck are you doing?" I say.

He runs his eyes over me, as if I've encouraged this, as if I want this. "Don't play coy Eden."

"The fuck does that mean?"

"I see you, the way you act, the way you are." He says. "Waltzing around in that little bikini of yours. You're a little slut just like your mother aren't you?"

My mouth drops. I don't know what to say. I think I'm frozen in shock. This is Dominic's Finance Director. His friend. What the fuck is going on right now?

"Come on, lie back, let me feel what goodies nature gave you and I'll give you a treat after." He murmurs.

"Fuck off." I half spit as I stumble back, getting out of the tub, feeling so sickened.

I head back to the house. In truth I want to run, to get away so fast but with everyone around us I don't want to make a scene, after all who would believe me? And more to the point even if they did I'd jeopardise Dominic's entire business. What he's spent years building. I can't do that. There's no way I can do that. No, better I keep my mouth shut and hope he takes the hint to leave me alone.

But when I walk into the house I can feel myself trembling anyway. I need a shower, I need to get clean. He might not have actually touched me but I feel so dirty right now and the word 'slut' keeps echoing in my head over and over.

"What are you doing?" My mother hisses.

I blink realising that she and Dominic are stood both staring at me. I shake my head, wrapping my arms around myself.

"You're dripping water everywhere." She snaps. "For god sake Eden do you have any sense? Didn't you think to use a towel?"

"I…" I gulp. Fuck I am stupid. Really stupid. I've messed up so much.

"Leave it alone." Dominic says to her. "It's just a bit of water."

"No it's not." My mother retorts. "She's making a mess everywhere. What will people think when they see this?"

"It's just a bit of water." Dominic growls.

She shakes her head and I see her eyes move for a moment in a way that tells me she's drunk. She always seems to be drinking these days, as if being at home drives her to it.

"Go dry yourself. And put something more decent on. Walking around dressed in next to nothing. You look like you're asking for it." She snarls and I flee then, biting back the tears, running from them both.

"Oh for god sake." I hear her say as if I'm the one being dramatic.

"I'll see if she's okay." Dominic says.

"I don't know why you bother. She's not worth your time Dominic…" My mother states.

He growls a reply but I can't hear them anymore. I'm too far up the stairs. Running to my room. Running to get away from the hate of her words.

I'm in the bathroom when I hear the tapping. I know it's him. I know he's just being kind but right now I don't think I want to see him. I don't know what I'd even say.

"Eden?" He says softly and I gasp because he's right outside the door, in my room now.

"Go away." I say feeling like a petulant child now.

"I'm going to come in." He says opening the door.

I half glare at him. I shouldn't even be angry at him but I am. I'm angry at everyone right now but I'm especially angry at myself.

"She didn't mean it." He says gently.

"Yes she did." I snap back.

"She's drunk."

"And I'm a slut." I reply.

He frowns. "What?"

"It's true isn't it? That's what everyone thinks."

He narrows his eyes. "No one thinks that Eden."

I scoff. "Yes they do. I see it in their faces, my mother said as much right now, and I know you think it."

"Why would I think that?"

I gulp. We're in dangerous ground now. Really dangerous ground. I glance at the door. He's shut it behind him. It's just us in, my bathroom, in the furthest corner of the house and I'm wearing the tiny bikini that's doing nothing to hide my body from his gaze.

"After what we did." I whisper it.

"You're not a slut." He says. "And that was my fault. I'm the adult here. I shouldn't have let that happen." He says but he's stepping closer not further away.

I take in a deep rattling breath as if to calm my nerves and in all honestly to try and calm the throbbing need that is pulsing in my core right now.

"I'm an adult too." I state.

He nods. "Yes you are but I'm in a position of authority. I took advantage."

I run my eyes over him, meeting his gaze and take the plunge. "What if I wanted you to take advantage again?" I say.

DOMINIC

Ten

She doesn't need to speak the words. I already know what she wants. I can see the way her nipples are showing through the red triangles of the top, I can see the way her pupils are dilating. She's turned on right now. She's horny.

And she wants me.

I can hear the voice in my head. Telling me to stop. Telling me this is a stupid idea. A stupid thing to do. That I have to stop.

But I don't.

My hands are on her thighs, skimming them as she bites her lip. She's not even doing it to be seductive, she's doing it subconsciously, as if it's a tick she has, a way of her body expressing her need.

I tug on the sides of her bikini where the strands hold it together and it comes apart so easily. She's not moving, she's not speaking, she's just watching me as I unwrap her for me.

As the fabric starts to fall I pull it away and she's there, standing half naked, taking long deep breaths as if she's trying not to lose control.

I pick her up, she's so light and she half wraps her legs around me as I place her onto the marble counter beside the sink. Her legs are open, her knees are bent and I've got the best angle of her cunt ever.

But I'm staring at her face, watching her reaction. I'm about to make another mistake, one I've been desperate to do for months, and while my wants are consuming me, I need to be sure she's consenting too. Because as much as I'm crossing a line, as much as I need my stepdaughter right now, I won't force her. If she tells me to stop, if she tells me to go, I'll turn around right now and not look back.

I owe her that much at least.

"Touch me." She says and I can feel she's trembling slightly. "Make me feel good."

I smirk slightly. "Oh don't worry about that." I murmur as my eyes drop to where her cunt is glistening with its welcome for me. "Daddy's going to make it all better."

She gasps, yeah me calling myself that turns her on.

I run my fingers down her, relishing the fact she's so smooth, that she's so wet too. My little angel is dripping just for me. She feels better than I imagined. Better than I hoped. She lets out a moan, a little sound that makes me do it again and her body secretes more juices.

I'm barely getting going and my little minx here is already so responsive. I plunge two fingers into her, pushing as hard as I can into her core and she groans as her eyes half pop out. I bet none of her little school boyfriends touched her like this. I bet no one has owned her cunt like this before.

She clings to me, her little muscles latching to my fingers as I pump. She's just so fucking malleable.

"Dominic." She gasps out my name and I grin. It's the first time she's said it in a moment like this and I realise that it won't be the last, that whatever the hell this is, now that we're here again we're going to keep on doing this, that this mistake will perpetuate, that we will continue for as long as we can, revelling in our sin, revelling in our damnation until we both burn.

Her cunt is squelching, slurping, with every move I make because of how wet she is and by god do I love that sound. She's flushing though, embarrassed and I make a point of doing it more, of making it louder which only makes her moan.

"That feel good sweetheart?" I say and she nods.

"So good."

"Do you want me to make you cum?"

"Yes." She says without hesitation. Without a moments pause.

I move my other hand to her clit and her eyes widen. My righthand fingers are still inside her. I use my left index and ring finger to spread her lips wider and my middle finger begins to circle. Slow deliberate movements around that little bundle of nerves I watched her manipulate to perfection all those months ago.

"Oh fuck." She says slamming her head back against the tiles.

I can't help it I chuckle at her reaction. "Bet those little boys you mess with have never made you feel like this huh?" I say.

She shakes her head.

"Tell your Daddy how good it is."

"It's so good. So good." She gasps. "Please don't stop."

"Oh I won't. I promise you Eden. I promise I'll take care of you and Daddy always keeps his promises doesn't he?"

"Yes." She moans so loudly I'm grateful we gave her this room, with this bathroom, grateful that we're far from where the party is happening right now and half our family are tucking into neatly cut sandwiches and making pathetic small talk.

She's moving her legs further apart, panting as her tits heave. I'm tempted to yank off her top and get a good look at them but both my hands are occupied and right now my focus is on her needs, her wants, not my own.

"I've wanted you to do this for months." She gasps. "I've been imagining it."

"Yeah?" I reply. She's sweating now. She's about to come undone. I can feel as her body starts to melt.

"I wanted you…" She trails off as her body jerks and then she's screaming, writhing, thrusting against me. I move my hand to cover her mouth. We might be away from the party but I'm not going to run the risk of us getting caught because I've been reckless.

"Dominic." She moans against my hand and it's the best fucking sound I've heard. Her juices are running down my fingers, down my wrist but she keeps going, as if her body isn't ready to give up just yet.

I push my body onto hers, using my size to try to stifle the sound, to soak it in.

When I feel her sink down I know she's done and I look at her face, meeting her eyes as she pants.

"Dominic." She whispers. "Please don't tell me that was another mistake."

I smirk, pulling my fingers out of her and as she watches I lick her juices from where they've run down my skin. Fuck she even tastes like heaven.

"Do you want it to be?" I ask.

She shakes her head.

"You want me to do it again?" I check.

"And more?" She asks.

I tilt my head. She's still sat wide open, exposed for me to look and even now she's dripping. "How much more?"

"As much as you'll give me." She says.

EDEN

Eleven

I stay in my room. I feign a headache when my mother comes looking for me and she's more than happy to buy the lie.

And I lay waiting, hoping, wondering where my stepfather is right now and if he's even thinking of me.

Fuck I hope he is.

Fuck I hope he really is because I want him to come back. I want him to continue. We've both thrown ourselves over the cliff now and I'm ready to fall the whole way down until we both crash on the rocks below.

"Eden?" He murmurs sticking his head through the door. "I bought you some food."

I sit up watching as he moves through the semi-darkness. The party was officially over ages ago but I can still hear my mother if I listen hard enough. I can hear other voices too.

"You didn't have to." I say.

He smirks. "No? Would you prefer I leave you to it then?"

"No." I say quickly. "Sit. Stay with me."

He winces like he's registered for a second what we're doing and then he does it. He perches on the edge of the bed, putting the plate between us.

"I didn't know what you wanted so I just grabbed some sandwiches."

I smile. He seems almost shy right now, uncertain and yet hours earlier he wasn't hesitating at all.

I lean over, switch the lamp on and we both blink as our eyes adjust.

And then I pick up a sandwich and eat. In truth I'm starving but nothing on this plate would satisfy my hunger.

He sighs watching me for a moment.

"Aren't you hungry?" I ask him.

He smirks. "Not for this."

"Something else?" I half whisper.

His eyes flash and I know we're both on the same page. That he wants more. That he's thinking about taking more.

"I couldn't stop thinking about you." I say.

He meets my eyes but he doesn't reply.

"I couldn't stop thinking about your dick."

His jaw shifts. His throat bops.

I put the plate aside, clear the space. He's watching me, as if he wants me to make the first move. I toss the duvet off me and his eyes drop immediately to where I'm sat, with my legs open, knees bent, in just a thong and t-shirt.

"Even when I tried not to." I say sliding my hand under the lace fabric. "Even when I tried to think of anyone else." I moan as I touch myself. "I just kept seeing your face."

He groans, grabbing my legs, yanking me down and I pull the lace fabric away so that he can watch.

"I wanted you to make me cum that day." I say. My legs are splayed wide. I'm thrusting as I pleasure myself and I love the fact that he's watching, enjoying every second of this.

"I was so horny and I wanted you to feel it, to feel how wet I was."

"Eden." He says. He's moving on top of me now. His body held over mine. "If we do this there's no going back."

"I don't want to go back." I say. "I've already told you that."

He groans. "You're my stepdaughter."

"And I want you." I state.

He shakes his head before lowering his face to mine. I can feel his stubble, I can feel the softness of his lips as he kisses me gently. Lovingly. I part my lips and his tongue slips in. Fuck he knows how to kiss, he really knows how to. He takes his time, caressing my tongue, exploring my mouth and I moan against him.

I'm not masturbating anymore though my hand is still on my pussy.

I'm too lost in his kiss to think of doing anything else.

He pulls away, staring into my eyes and I blush as I look back.

And then slowly, his hands find the bottom of my t-shirt and he starts pulling it up.

I'm not wearing a bra. I'm not wearing anything under it and his eyes widen as he stares at my breasts.

My breath is coming so fast. My chest is rising and falling and I can feel my nipples hardening more and more.

His hands drop to cup me and I shut my eyes feeling the contrast of his warm hands, of the way he's touching me so softly with his hard, calloused skin.

"Fuck Eden." He groans. Stroking them, teasing them, practically worshipping them. He lowers his lips to my left and he sucks my nipple in.

"Oh shit." I cry.

"Ssssh." He murmurs. "We have to be quiet."

"I don't want to be." I say back.

He sighs. "This time you have too."

"I want you to make me scream."

He grins. "Don't worry about that because you will be soon enough."

He sucks again, his tongue wrapping around as he rolls my nipple before gently nibbling on it. The man is incredible. His mouth is a portal to heaven and I want him to possess every piece of me.

He drags him thumb over it, scratching it, making it so hard as he turns his attention to my right breast.

"Your tits are incredible." He says.

"They're yours. Every piece of me is yours." I say.

He grins. "Every piece?"

"Every piece you want."

He tilts his head, grabbing my breast going suddenly rabid as he loses himself.

I moan, I writhe, I wrap my legs around his body and I can feel his dick. Even now I can feel how hard he is.

"My naughty little stepdaughter." He says.

I giggle for a moment but it catches in my throat as I feel his hands moving to my where mine is, between my thighs.

"You're wet." He says. "So wet."

"Wet for you Daddy." I reply.

He smirks, pulling my hand away shifting so that he has a better view of my pussy.

"This cunt needs proper attention." He says.

I nod. Yes she does.

"Not the pathetic teasing you just did." He states.

My jaw drops. "I wasn't…"

He silences me with a look. "I'm going to make you cum again Eden. I'm going to show you what it feels like when a man touches you."

I nod. I've already experienced his kind of attention and I'm ready for more.

"I'm going to teach this pussy so many tricks she'll never want to be touched by those little boys you mess around with anymore."

"I only want to be touched by you."

He raises an eyebrow. "Is that so?" He spreads my labia wide, exposing all of my inner flesh for him to see.

"You've got a very pretty cunt did you know that?"

I blush. I like that he likes it. Not that I really have any control over how I look but still.

He touches my clit. Strokes it for a second and I feel my body respond by getting wetter.

"So responsive." He murmurs.

He starts circling, lightly, teasingly, I leak out more juices and he grins, enjoying as I fight my urge to move, my urge to writhe, my need for him to keep this going.

"When you cum you say my name, you hear me?" He says. I nod. I love how domineering he is. How controlling too. "You cum for me."

"I cum for you." I reply as he picks up speed, as he starts manipulating my body, forcing me to hurtle towards my conclusion.

"Dominic." I gasp but I'm not cuming yet. I just need to affirm to myself that this is real, that this is happening, that I've not fallen into some crazy dream and I'll wake in a hot needy mess without him.

"Ssssh." He murmurs. "Trust me and I'll give you everything you want."

"I want you." I say. "I only want you."

He grins and his fingers send me over the edge, I shudder, I jerk, his body holds me as the coil inside me snaps and I have to bury my face in the pillow to stop my screams. But we both hear it anyway. We both hear his name on my lips.

"Good girl." He says as I fall to pieces beneath him. He brushes the hair from my face. "That's a good girl." He says in a way that makes it sound like we're done here. Like he's given me my reward and now it's over.

"Don't go." I say.

"I'm not."

"Stay with me tonight."

He sighs. "I can't."

DOMINIC

Twelve

I see her face fall. I know its stupid reckless to even be here right now but to stay in her room? Hell I'm asking to get caught.

I stare down, her t-shirt is up by her throat, her tits are out and my mouth is watering now at how they hang. They're bigger than I imagined, than I realised. She's got a woman's body. But then I knew she wasn't a child.

I can feel her cum on my fingers. I can taste her on my tongue.

And in my pants, my cock is throbbing so hard I don't know how I haven't exploded everywhere already.

"Please Dominic." She says.

"Give me a moment." I reply. Getting up walking away when all I really want to do is sink my cock into her and make myself at home.

I walk out, tucking my erection under my belt and pulling my shirt out to cover any last traces.

Somewhere in my house my wife is no doubt still drinking.

I stalk through the hallway. Most of the family left hours ago. Timothy stalked off at some point. There's only Terri and a few of her work friends left.

I find them sat in the garden, her, her boss and two others I don't really know.

"Dom." She says smiling.

"I'm going to head to bed." I say.

She nods. "You don't mind if we carry on?" She slurs.

"Not at all." I say. "Enjoy yourselves. I'll sleep in the spare room so you can come in whenever."

She smiles glancing at everyone as if she's trying to make a show of what a great husband I am and I feel a pang of something at the fact her daughters cum is still all over my fingertips.

"Well goodnight everyone." I say.

"Goodnight." They murmur and I leave them to it. Job done.

I head back inside, heading to the room I usually crash in and I make a mess of the bed so it looks like it's been slept in. Just in case someone checks. Only I know they won't. Terri will be too hungover. She'll stay in bed most of tomorrow so if I play my cards right I'll be able to keep Eden occupied all through the morning.

I shake my head. It's almost unnerving how easily I'm slipping into the role of the deceitful husband. I should feel more guilty. I should feel more concern but I don't.

I walk back into Eden's room. She's sat waiting for me. Her t-shirt is on the floor now. She's discarded it completely and I'm curious to see if she's done the same with that skimpy thong too.

"All sorted." I say.

"Seriously?" She gasps.

"Did you doubt me?"

She shakes her head. "Not for a minute."

I laugh. Of course my little minx didn't. I start undoing my shirt and her eyes drop. She's never seen me topless, I've always been too conscious of crossing lines to walk around the house in anything less than full clothes though I recognise the irony of that now.

"You're…?" She says staring at my body.

"Ripped?" I say and she giggles. "What did you expect? Some wizened old man?" I murmur moving to the bed. I know I'm in good shape. I work out a lot. It's a good stress relief amongst other things and these last few months this girl has been stressing me out more than anything else.

She gulps. Perhaps I'm moving too fast. The way her body is trembling right now seems to suggest it and despite my want to charge into whatever this is headfirst my need to care for her overrides everything.

"We won't do anything you don't want to." I say.

She nods shifting, pulling the covers up so that I can get in and I see she's still wearing the thong after all. It must be drenched by now. Soaked in her juices.

As I lie down she curls into me running her hand over my skin. Her fingertips are cold but the sensation feels so good. She traces along my tattoos as if she can't quite match them to me but she must have seen at least the ones on my arm because it's not exactly like my t-shirt hides them.

"You're so warm." She says.

"I'm a hot blooded man." I state.

She bites her lip and slowly, she raises her head and kisses me. Her hands wrap in my hair, she moans as she does it and I can feel as her body leans further into me.

Instinctively I grab her, pulling her in and my hands find her tits. She arches her back, clearly enjoying as I start to manipulate them.

And then I feel her hands on me, touching me, feeling my body, tickling at my chest hair before she moves lower. I'm still wearing my trousers. I haven't taken them off and as she reaches for my belt I let her do it.

If she wants to fuck then I sure as hell won't stop her but I'm going to let her make the final call.

I slide them off after she's undone them but I keep my boxers on. Her hands fumble to feel me and I groan.

"I like your dick." She says as she starts palming it through the fabric. Getting me more excited. "I like the feel of it."

"That's good because it likes you too."

She smiles, sliding her hand under the elastic and taking hold of me as if she knows what she's doing.

"Would Daddy like to cum too?" She says and my cock jerks with excitement.

"So much so." I reply.

She licks her lips and I realise she's not going to jack me off, she's going to suck me again. Lord have mercy.

She rolls over on top of me, the duvet covers her and I pull it away. I won't have anything taking away the view I have right now.

Her tits are hanging perfectly. She's curled up over my groin, staring at me like my cock is her salvation. Like it holds everything she'll ever need.

"Put it in your mouth and suck it like a good girl." I say.

She nods, pulling my cock up and puckers her lips, gliding me in.

And fuck do I groan then. I don't even care if they catch us in this moment. I don't even care who hears. Her mouth is incredible. Her tongue can perform miracles. She's taking me, sucking me, letting me slide down her throat as if she doesn't even have a gag reflex, as if her mouth was solely designed for my cock.

I buck against her, she gasps a bit but still no choke. My perfect fucking angel.

She takes her time, she works me up till I'm so close to cuming it hurts and then she slows right now. She's playing a few tricks of her own I realise and I grin because I want to find out what more she can do.

"Don't be a tease." I murmur.

"No? Daddy doesn't like that?"

"No." I say.

She lowers her mouth, licking me, sucking me slowly before pulling off again. "Would you spank me?"

"Excuse me?"

"Would you spank me, if I'm naughty?" She asks before licking along the length of me and battering her eyelashes.

I narrow my eyes. I'm not sure if this is just sex talk or if she really means it.

She licks again. "Daddy?"

"Do you want to be spanked?" I ask.

She nods, taking my cock once more, sliding her delicious tongue all over it. "Yes." She says. "I want you to punish me when I'm naughty."

"And reward you when you're good?" I say.

"Yes." She says before sucking more, turning her full attention to my cock as if it is her reward and she's ready for it now.

I groan, shutting my eyes, placing my hand on her head as she works away.

"I'm going to cum." I groan. "I'm going to cum down your throat and that will be your reward for tonight."

She moans, she pumps away at the base of me and I jerk, growling as my balls clench and I pour into her warm perfect little mouth.

She swallows it all, licking her lips as if she's never tasted anything as good and I pull her up to lie beside me again.

We should sleep. That's what a voice in my head says. We need to sleep. It must be four in the morning by now. Thank fuck it's the weekend and I have nothing else to do tomorrow.

Eden lays beside me and without thinking I start circling her nipples. She gasps but she lays there still, letting me play, letting me enjoy her body.

"Would it turn you on to be spanked?" I ask her.

"If you spanked me." She says.

"Not anyone else?"

She shakes her head.

"What about bondage? Handcuffs?" I ask. I've never been that into BDSM. I've never got the pain aspect but hell if my little Lolita here is up for it then I'm willing to give it a try.

"I'm not sure." She says.

"Okay, just a little spanking then." I murmur.

"And only when I'm naughty."

"Are you planning on being naughty Eden?" I ask her and she blushes.

Her nipples are so hard right now. They're poking out enough that I can properly tweak the middle and I make a point of pinching them.

She jerks but I can tell she likes it.

"I'm a good girl Daddy. You know that." She says.

Yeah she is. My stepdaughter. My perfect fucking angel.

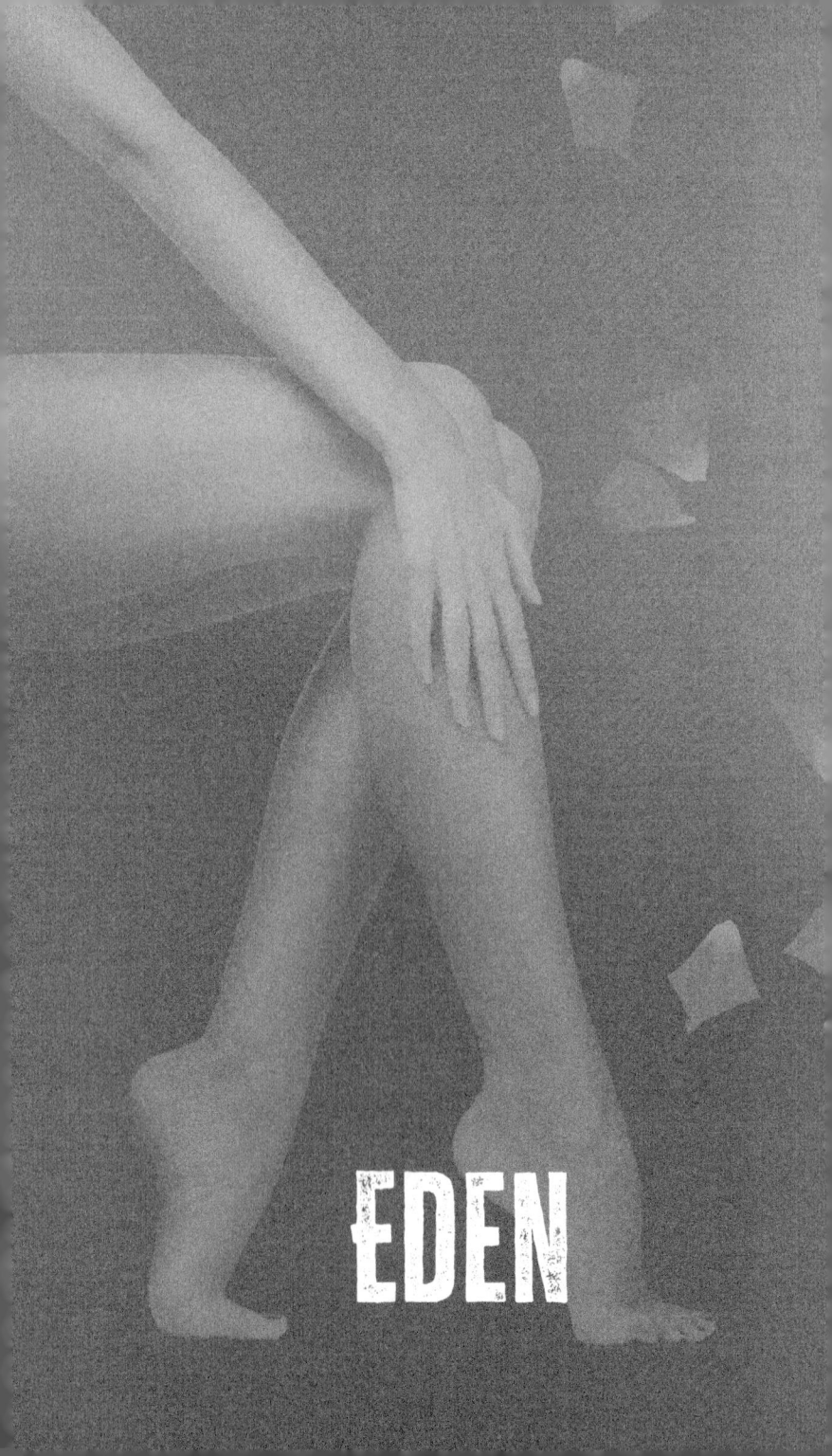

EDEN

Thirteen

The party was days ago. Between work shifts and homework I've not seen Dominic since.

And to say I'm missing him is an understatement.

Every time I shut my eyes I dream of him and I wake up so horny I've had to masturbate so many times I've lost count and I swear I'm wearing the batteries out on the bullet vibrator.

I'm also ignoring all calls from Aron because I don't know how to deal with him. I mean it's clear that we're over. It was over before I started messing with Dominic but when I think about the technicalities, the fact that I've essentially cheated, it makes me more than a little uncomfortable. But then Dominic's not exactly a free agent either. God this is complicated.

My mother walks in, her high heels clack on the marble as she walks towards me.

I look up from my laptop and smile.

"Are you busy right now?" She says.

"I'm working on an essay."

"So not busy then." She says.

"Do you want me to do something?" I ask. What's the point in arguing anyway? She'll only win like all the other times.

"Yes as a matter of fact." She says. "Dominic left some files here and he needs them. I've got an important meeting in…" She looks at her sparkling Rolex for dramatic effect. "In less than an hour."

"So you want me to take him the files?"

"Yes." She says as if I'm stupid. "Can you manage it?"

"Sure." I reply. Ignoring the feeling already billowing inside me at the thought of having a legitimate reason to see him right now.

"Well get on with it then. He's a busy man. He doesn't have time to wait on the whims of a silly girl." She says like I'm an idiot.

"Where are they?" I ask.

"Where are what?" She huffs.

"The files he needs."

"In his office. On his desk." She says before walking off.

I shake my head, shutting my laptop and get up. If I had more time I'd put some makeup on, make a bit of an effort but I know I look hot enough already and besides I don't want any random observers to see something in my behaviour that gives me away.

I walk down past the kitchen, past the dining room and to where his office is. I never really go in here. I don't have any reason too. It's neat, organised. Everything is in its place. Even the files are stacked with precision on his desk.

For a second an idea hits me and I grin deciding to do it despite the risk. I rub my thong along me, making sure it's good and covered then slip it off, curling it up and pop it into one of his drawers. A little present for him to find later.

And then I scoop up the files and head out to my car.

When I pull up to his office, they tell me he's at the new construction site and though a part of me knows I could reasonably leave the files at HQ it feels like I should give them to him in person. He's a busy man after all.

I sigh getting into my car, mentally writing off what was going to be a good few hours of essay writing and drive across the city to where he no doubt is waiting.

When I pull up I feel eyes on me. The place is alive with workmen, bricklayers, chippies, they're all there, in hard hats and in the distance the sound of heavy machinery reverberates. Half the men are topless as if it's so hot they have to be getting it all out.

I pick up the files and get out, grateful now that I haven't made more of an effort because I feel conspicuous enough as it is in my tennis dress and plimsols.

Someone calls out. I frown looking round. But I don't recognise them.

Another wolf-whistles as if we're not in the twenty first century, as if feminism never even happened.

"Fuck sake." I mutter under my breath because I don't have the balls to berate them.

"Where's Dominic Mathers?" I ask as a man, a labourer walks past. He gives me a funny look then nods his head behind him.

Only there's no one there, just a load of scaffolding.

"Hey pretty, who you looking for?" Someone says leaning over the scaffolding bars above me.

"Not you Malcs." Someone else says laughing.

"Nah no one wants your cock, wrinkly old thing that it is." Another shouts.

They all laugh while I'm stood feeling like an idiot as my face flushes with embarrassment.

"What the fuck is this?" Dominic growls as he stalks towards us. They all fall silent as they see his face looking like thunder.

"Do you think it's okay to harass women?" He snaps as they make themselves busy. And then he turns his attention to me. "What are you doing here?" He asks in a way that makes me flinch.

"I brought the files you needed." I say holding them up as if they're my defence. "Mum said you needed them urgently."

"Fucking hell." He grumbles. "I asked her to bring them. Can she not even do a single thing…" He trails off.

"Come on." He jerks his head, turning, and heads back the way he comes, expecting me to follow. And I do, admiring his ass as much as I can get away with in the jeans he's got on.

He climbs the stairs to a cabin, holds the door without even looking at me and then lets it go the minute I'm inside. "Put them on my desk will you." He says waiving a hand not looking at me still.

I walk over putting them down and huff.

"Are you not even going to say thanks?" I reply.

He sighs, pouring out a mug of coffee. "It's been a long day."

"Yeah?" I reply. "Sounds real tough."

I go to leave and he grabs my arm. "I'm sorry. I don't mean to be a shit."

"I'm just trying to help." I say.

"I know that." He says pulling me closer to him. "You're a good girl."

I raise an eyebrow. Is he seriously pulling that right now?

"Not like that." He says. "I didn't mean like that."

"What did you mean?" I ask annoyed.

"I mean that bringing these files is helpful. Thank you."

"You're welcome." I reply only he's not letting me go. He's staring right at me. "Dominic?"

"I've missed you." He says. His hands are scooting around my back, reaching down as he goes to grope my ass.

"Dominic." I say.

"I wondered if you were second guessing this, avoiding me even." He says.

"You mean like you did after I sucked you off the first time?" I say and he grins.

"You knew about that?"

"It was kind of obvious." I murmur. He's squeezing my ass, massaging it. "And I'm not avoiding you. I've just been busy. I've had coursework, assignments and work work."

"So quit."

"Excuse me?"

"Quit your job. You don't need it anyway. I give you enough of an allowance." He says leaning back against the coffee stand behind.

"I don't want your money…."

"I know, you're an independent woman." He says in a way that makes me laugh.

"I've been putting every penny you give me aside. I'm going to pay it all back with my college tuition as well."

"You don't need too."

"I want too."

"Eden, will you just let me take care of you."

"You already do." I say smirking.

He grins more. "Let Daddy take care of you." He says. "Let me treat you."

I bite my lip. "Talking of treats, I left you one in your office at home."

He raises an eyebrow. "What?"

"You'll have to wait and see."

"I'm not a patient man." He murmurs, pulling at my dress, raising it.

"Maybe you should learn to be."

"And where would be the fun in that?" He says as he gives it one final tug and his eyes widen as he sees I'm not wearing anything underneath. "Where are your panties?"

"In your office. At home." I state.

He lets out a laugh. "And here I was thinking you'd gone off me." He says sliding his fingers between my lips, teasing me as I moan.

"Why would I?" I manage to half gasp.

He shrugs. "I'm more than twice your age. Maybe you had your fun…" He says as he starts circling my entrance, probing it rather than penetrating it.

"With age comes experience." I say. "Maybe that's what I like."

He smirks. "You like my experience?" He says as he finally grants me some mercy and sinks two fingers in.

"Yes." I gasp more loudly than I should.

"My little Lolita likes the way this old man uses her body?"

I nod, biting my lip. Fuck I'm going to cum and he's barely even gotten started. I don't even know how he's doing it. How he's able to have such a devastatingly delicious effect but I know I don't want him to stop. I never want him to stop.

"Old man." I moan. "Such an old man."

He grins. I know he can hear it. I know he can see it too.

"You're about to cum aren't you?" He says as I shift my feet, as I move my hands to grip him.

"Dominic." I shudder.

"Cum for me Eden. Cum for your Daddy."

I nod, I shudder again and then I throw my head back letting it wash over me, letting my body do what it so desperately needs to as Dominic watches on like a man possessed. I can only hope the sound of the machine outside drowns out the sound of my screams but Dominic slaps his hand over my mouth stifling them as best he can.

I fall into this chest and he pulls my dress back down. "That's my thank you for the files."

"You're such a shit." I murmur and his chest vibrates as he laughs.

"Careful Eden, I might decide to wash that potty mouth of yours out."

I step back, trying not to stare at his crotch because I know what I'll see if I do and the last thing I need right now is him trying to fuck me because, in the state I'm in, I doubt I'd even put up much of defence.

"Dom, have you got…?" Timothy pauses looking between us. "Sorry Eden, I didn't realise you were here." He looks at Dominic with a more than quizzical expression.

"She was just dropping off the Addison files." Dominic says grabbing the coffee mug and walking round to sit at his desk.

"Well, now that I've done my job I'll head home." I say. "My essay won't write itself."

"No it won't." Dominic replies as if he's not the reason I'm almost certainly going to be pulling an all-nighter now.

I don't look at Timothy as I walk past. I hope my reaction back in the hot tub was enough for him to get the message and anyway I don't care much what he thinks of me. It's Dominic's opinion that concerns me and he's just made it abundantly clear that he likes me just as I am.

DOMINIC

Fourteen

I watch her go sipping my coffee. If my raging erection could just go as easily then I'd be more than happy with the turn of events.

"Dom." Tim says as he pulls up a chair.

"Coffee's just brewed." I state.

"Nah I'm good." He replies before glancing back as if he's still expecting Eden to be here. "What was she doing here?"

"Like I said just dropping off these files." I reply picking them up.

"You've got her running errands for you now?" He laughs.

"Not errands." I reply. "Terri was meant to bring them but she was too busy."

He snorts. "Course she was." He mutters. "Still not a bad substitute."

"Meaning?" I say tilting my head. That's my fucking stepdaughter he's talking about.

"Come on man, don't act like you've not whacked one out over her."

"The fuck are you talking about?" I growl.

"Eden. She's a hot bit of stuff. Who hasn't had a wank to the thought of her?"

I shake my head, my anger is flashing and it's all I can do not to throw this desk aside and beat the living shit out of the man.

"You and I are going to have a serious falling out if you don't watch how you speak about Eden." I state.

"Sorry mate." He says but he doesn't look like it. "You two looked pretty cosy anyway."

"Meaning?"

"Meaning you sure you're not being overly protective for reasons other than being her stepdad?"

I snarl. "I took her on, helped raised her from the age of thirteen."

He nods like he doesn't know it. Like this is new information. While I try not to think about the fact I'm literally fucking around with her, the girl I should look upon as my kid. The girl I do look upon as my kid.

"What did you want?" I ask sitting back in my chair.

"The new accounts we filed. The auditors found a discrepancy."

"What sort of discrepancy?" I ask.

"There's a quarter million missing."

"What? From where?"

"Here." He says laying the paper down and showing me the highlighted sections. "These are all the transactions we can't account for."

I run my hand over my face. "Are you saying what I think you're saying?"

"That someone is stealing from the fund? Yeah that's exactly it."

"Fuck." I hiss. No one even has access but me and Timothy and a handful of others. "We have to get the police involved."

"No we don't. Not until we know what's what."

"The longer we wait, the more suspicious this looks." I state.

"And if it is nothing then we've caused a whole heap of shit for nothing."

"Fuck." I groan. He's got a point but that doesn't mean I think he's right.

"Leave it with me." He says. "I'll get it sorted."

I nod and he gets up and goes.

But as soon as he's gone I pull my phone out and call a police contact anyway. I'll be damned if I let my own stupid mistakes bring the entire company down and if there is a thief, which it's more than likely there is, I want them caught, I want them held accountable. I want them brought to justice.

EDEN

Fifteen

When I get home I'm relieved to find mum's not back. That the house is empty.

I head up to my room, taking a shower, needing to clean myself after making such a mess in Dominic's office. I take the opportunity to wash my hair too. It's normally so unruly that I leave it as long as possible but if I wash it now I won't have to bother drying it which is a definite bonus on the frizz front.

When I'm clean, I pull on a pair of joggers and a hoody, and go sit back in the snug, where I left my laptop and spend what feels like hours constructing my essay. Adding in my sources, making sure I cite the references correctly and that above all I've drawn conclusions that fit my argument and don't steer it in another direction.

It's not a bad essay considering. It's not my best if I'm honest but it could be a lot worse too.

It's late when I decide to put some pizza on. I expected mum to come home and yet it's still just me. Alone.

I scoff the food down, not caring if I make a mess. My mother would be making comments right now about my eating habits, about the lack of veggies, about the carbs, but it's not like I'm fat and besides, I like pizza.

When I'm done I chuck the plate in the dishwasher and head back to my essay, burying myself in it for a few more hours.

I wonder where Dominic is too. Perhaps they've gone out together and though the thought makes me jealous I disregard it because they've not been like that, gone on a date by themselves in years. It's like they live separate lives. If you didn't know they were married you certainly wouldn't guess it from the way they are most of the time.

Maybe that's why I don't feel as guilty as I should. Maybe that's why I don't care that Dominic is my stepdad.

Maybe.

I hear the door click and someone walking about but I don't look up. I'm tucked away anyway so it's not like I'm being deliberately antisocial and this essay isn't going to proofread itself.

"Hey you."

I look up at his voice. And I'm alarmed by how much my heart leaps.

"Hi." I say back.

He looks tired. He looks a little worn out if I'm honest.

"What are you working on?" He asks.

"Just an essay." I say.

"Yeah?" He murmurs sitting down. "Tell me about it."

"About my essay?" I laugh.

"Yeah. I'm interested."

"Okay." I say. "It's about Paradise Lost and whether Milton is intentional in making the protagonist likeable as a testament to the temptations of evil."

He smiles like he understands but I can see from his face he has no idea what the hell I'm talking about.

"You do what 'Paradise Lost' is right?"

He shakes his head and I laugh.

"Seriously? It's a twelve book epic poem written by a blind man. It's a work of genius or heresy depending on how you interpret it."

"Read me some." He says.

"Read you some of Paradise lost?"

He nods.

"Why?"

"I want to hear it."

I bite my lip. He's messing with me. I know it. But what the hell.

"Alright." I say, pulling out my notes.

"No, from heart."

"What?"

"Tell me a bit that sticks with you. That you remember."

"What is this some chat up line?"

He narrows his eyes. "Tell me Eden."

"Fine." I murmur. "The mind is its own place. It can make a heaven of hell or a hell of heaven." I say hoping I got it right but it's not like he'll really know anyway.

"You really like books?" He says.

"I like reading."

He nods. "So what do you want to do with this degree, what do you want to do after?"

"I don't know." I say. "I kind of…" I trail off. For some reason it feels more personally to be having this conversation with him, as if it means more, spilling my secrets, telling him the one thing I aspire to be when I've never admitted it to another human being before. Never truly admitted it to myself either.

"Kind of what?" He asks.

"Promise you won't laugh." I say.

"I won't."

"I want to be a writer. I want to create something. Something that outlives me."

He's staring at me like I'm something amazing. "You can be a writer if that's what you want Eden."

I scoff. Like it's easy.

"Whatever you want to be, you can achieve it, if you work hard." He says.

"What about you? I doubt you wanted to be what you are growing up." I say.

He smiles. "I knew I'd run my own business. I can't explain how, I just knew it."

"Did you know it would be in construction, property development?"

"Yeah. It's all I could do. I was good with my hands. I started off as a brickie. I worked from the ground up."

"And now look at you." I say.

He smiles. "Doing alright."

"Yeah I'd say that." I reply.

He leans over and sweeps my hair from where it's hanging over my shoulder.

"And I'm still good with my hands." He says.

"Is that another chat up line?" I laugh.

"Do you want it to be?"

"Where's mum?" I ask. I hate to ask but if there's any chance of her being around I'm not doing anything.

"She's working."

"At this hour?" I scoff.

He smirks. "Apparently some client is in and it was all hands to the deck with smoozing them."

"Wow."

"Yeah I'd say that. Still…" He pulls my face to look at him fully. "It does give us a little alone time."

"Is that what you want?" I ask.

"Don't you?"

I shrug. It's hard to deny I don't want him right now, hell my core is practically screaming for him and yet I don't just want to be a thing he fucks, a thing he sees as entertainment when his wife isn't around.

"What are you thinking Eden?" He says quietly.

I let out a low sigh. "I want you." I say. "But I also don't want to just be a bit of fun."

He raises his eyebrows, opens his mouth to reply but I talk over him.

"I get this is complicated, I get that you can't exactly take me out, wine and dine me like I'm a normal date but I also don't want this just to be physical."

"I don't want just physical either." He says. "Although it's hard to deny I'm not attracted to your body, that I'm not desperate to rip your clothes off, I like you as a person. And I want to get to know you more."

"I've lived with you for eight years." I state. "Don't you know me well enough?"

He chuckles. "As a daughter maybe but I don't want to look at you and think that."

"I am your stepdaughter." I say.

"And I don't really care Eden." He states. "I want to charm you. To treat you right."

I sigh. "What about mum?"

"What about her?" He asks.

I hesitate, I'm in dangerous territory now. Crossing Line. "Would you leave her?"

He narrows his eyes. "Eden…"

"I'm not asking you too. Not right now but if we have any chance of a future together then I need to know that you'll do it one day."

"You want a future with me?" He says.

"Don't you?"

He blinks. "You're twenty one Eden. I'm forty two. I doubt you'll want to spend the prime years of your life with some old duffer."

"You're not an old duffer."

"No?" He says smirking.

"No." I reply. "And you don't know what I want."

He sighs. "Look neither of us knows what the future holds. I'm not saying I won't leave your mum but I'm also not denying that you wouldn't change your mind at some point about what we're doing. About whether you want us to continue."

"So what…?"

"How about we don't make plans? How about we just see where this goes for the moment?"

I hate to admit it but my heart sinks a little as he says it. It feels like he's trying to fob me off. That this is just a bit of fun to him, that I'm just a bit of fun.

"I'm not saying I don't see a future Eden. I'm just saying things are complicated, really complicated and I don't want to set us up to fail."

I nod. "Okay."

He pulls me to him, wrapping his arms around me as we lie back on the couch.

"I liked seeing you today. I liked you coming to the office." He says.

"You mean cuming in your office." I say.

He laughs. "Yeah I liked that too."

"What did Timothy want?" I don't know why I ask it, I shouldn't care but that man sets me on edge.

He pulls a face but his body tenses. "Just some stuff with work."

"What is it?" I ask.

His face goes serious. "Nothing you need to worry about."

"You can trust me, you know that?"

He smiles. "Yeah. I know."

"Then tell me. Maybe I can help."

He leans in, his hot breath hits my face and I can smell the peppermint on it. God I'm dying to kiss him right now, to stick my tongue deep in his mouth and taste it. "You want to help?"

I nod. "I do."

I can see the glint in his eyes. I can see where this is headed already and while a part of me wants to be serious the other part is saying that we're here, alone, and right now we can make as much noise as we want.

DOMINIC

Sixteen

"Take off your clothes then." The words are out of my mouth before I realise I've even spoken them.

She hesitates for the minutest of seconds and then she's up, pulling her hoody off, pulling her tank top off, sliding her joggers down.

I let out a low whistle as she stands in just her bra and thong. Waiting as if for my approval.

"And the rest." I say. "Show Daddy that beautiful body of yours."

She blushes but she does it. Unhooking her bra, letting it fall and as she leans over to slide her thong down I get the best view of her tits. I'm seeing her completely naked in full lighting for the first time and god is she beautiful.

"Now you." She says.

I tilt my head. "You want me naked too?"

"It seems only fair." She states. Yeah it does. Something tells me that tonight we might be taking this up a notch. Raising the stakes.

I unbutton my shirt, drop my pants. I'm not as sexy, as seductive in my movements as Eden, but the way she's watching me says she's still into it.

"I didn't realise you had so many tattoos." She murmurs stepping closer, running her hand over the one on my thigh that she's clearly only just noticed.

I smirk. "Do you like them?" Her mother definitely doesn't.

She nods. "They suit you."

I take a moment to study her, her perfect olive skin, the way her waist and hips curve. She stands perfectly still, letting my run my hands over her, letting me explore her body, touch where I want.

She's got a small scar on her side. I run my fingers over it feeling the raised skin.

"The appendicitis." She murmurs and I nod. I remember it, not long after me and Terri had got together, she'd been so sick, she was rushed to hospital and for a few moments I didn't know if she'd make it. I cradled her in my arms while Terri seemed frozen unable to do anything.

She'd been so fragile then, so small too. A tiny slip of a child. Not like the woman she is stood naked before me right now.

Her hands find a scar on me. A deep nasty one.

"How did you get that?"

I frown. "That's a story for another time."

She frowns too and then I pick her up, spin her around and put her face first on top of the table.

"Dominic." She gasps.

I grab her hips, yanking her perfect arse up into the air and she actually starts to quiver.

My hand strikes her left cheek and she gasps more. I can see the mark, the flush of pink. I hit her again on her right.

"Oh fuck." She says.

"You've been a naughty girl Eden." I say.

"How?"

"Coming to my office with no panties on, did you want me to fuck you?"

She murmurs something but it gets lost as I spank her more. Fuck the way my hand feels on her ass is incredible.

"Were you hoping I'd sink my cock into you for all the workmen to see?" I say.

"No." She says and I laugh staring at where her cunt is so perfectly angled for me if I wanted to take her.

She's so wet she's practically dripping. I guess she does like getting spanked and if I'm honest I like spanking her. I like playing the dominant just a little. Just for a moment.

I bend down, putting my mouth on her and she shudders.

Her cunt tastes so damn good. I roll my tongue over her. Savouring it.

"Oh fuck. Dominic…" She starts to squirm beneath me. I grab her head, holding her firmly in place by it.

"Let Daddy has his dinner sweetheart." I say before feasting once more.

She's so slick, so smooth, the fact she doesn't have any hair turns me on so much as I run my tongue between her folds, as I lick all over her, marking her with my saliva if you will.

"That's so good." She moans.

"Yeah?" I say lifting my face. "You like me eating you out?"

"I fucking love it." She says and I grin before getting right back to her.

Her cunt just keeps leaking out more and more juices. I tease her clit with my fingertips as my tongue starts to probe her arsehole.

"Have you ever done anal Eden?"

She freezes for a second and that tells me everything I need to know.

"I…" Her words falter and die as I start licking, sucking her arsehole.

"Fuck Daddy. Fuck." She says and I grin. She's loving this.

I plunge my fingers into her cunt and she jolts but my hand holds her.

"Take what Daddy gives you." I say pumping away, working her up, feeling as she starts to heave, as she starts to really make a noise and then she's screaming, cuming as I stand over her, enjoying every second of it.

I pull my fingers out. Give her a moment to get her breath back and then I'm grabbing my dick, probing her tight little hole with it.

She freezes but I don't really register it. If I'm honest I'm too lost in my own pleasure right now, too lost in the thought of how fucking incredible she's going to feel wrapped around me. How fucking fantastic this is going to be to finally sink my cock into her.

"Wait." She says. "Wait, wait, wait."

I stop, letting go of her hair and she rolls over staring up at me. I realise suddenly that I've gone too fast. I'm moving too fast. Way too fast.

"It's okay." I say. "We're doing this at your pace."

She nods. "I want to, I just…I'm not ready."

"I can wait. For as long as you need."

She thanks me as if she's not used to someone saying that and the thought pisses me off. She deserves to be treated with respect. And clearly from the look on her face she's not had that from the schoolboy pricks she's been with before.

She's blushing staring at me. And then she leans forward, grabbing my cock, pumping it slowly with her hand. She's clearly not done yet. She still wants more of me and if I have to spend the entire night making her cum with just my fingers I'm happy to do it.

"Would you, would you cum on me?" She says.

"What?"

"Cum on me. Cum all over me."

I fight back the grin. "Would you like that?"

"Yeah. I want you to cover me in it."

Fuck. I've never had someone actually asked me to do that. I mean sure I'm into it but most women don't like the mess.

She lays back, spreading herself wider in anticipation as if she's about to be baptised by me.

"Touch yourself." I say. "Touch yourself while Daddy watches and if you're good you'll get your reward."

She nods, grinning, yeah she's as into this as me right now. Her hands move to her cunt. She does what I did when I touched her and she uses one to spread lips wide for me.

"Such a pretty cunt." I say, taking hold of my cock. My balls are aching to be emptied but I want to make this last. Make sure we both enjoy this to the max.

She starts masturbating with the other hand, I watch as I slowly pump away.

She's slow, teasing, her movements are different to mine. She's only focused on her clit.

"Don't you stick your fingers in?" I ask.

She shakes her head. "No. It doesn't do anything."

I let out a laugh because she cums readily enough when I'm penetrating her.

"Stick them in, curl them inside." I say.

She stares at me as she does it.

"Slowly, find that spot in you that you like."

"Oh fuck."

"There you go sweetheart."

"Fuck that's…"

"Better?"

She nods, biting her lip. Yeah she fucking loves that.

"I told you Daddy would teach you all the right tricks."

"Cum on me. Please." I can hear the need in her as she says it.

"I will." I say. I'm close but I want to watch a little longer. I've got this all planned out now in my head.

She's finger fucking herself, she's writhing. Her hands are moving so fast. My perfect little angel is giving me the best show of my life and as my precum oozes out I can't take my eyes from her.

"Dominic please." She gasps.

I pick up my pace, I want her to be screaming in her own ecstasy while she's covered in my cum.

"Eden." I groan as I feel my balls constrict, as my body tenses and I spurt shoots of jizz across her chest, across her body.

"Oh my god yes." She cries as if I've just blessed her.

I run my hands over, smearing it over her chest as she starts to writhe and flush. She's about to cum too. I can see it in her face. I've learnt the signs now. The way her brow furrows, the way her jaw locks for a second before everything relaxes and she melts into herself.

She screams. She screams so loudly. I stand watching, admiring, hell worshipping as my stepdaughter orgasms just for me.

Fuck she really is perfect. My little Lolita. My wanton angel.

"Dominic." She gasps. Her tits are heaving. She looks like she's never cum so hard in her life.

"Did you like that?" I say.

She laughs. "Yes. Did I help you?"

"Oh you did."

She stares down at herself, running a finger through the cum and then she puts it in her mouth sucking for a moment. And Jesus, if my balls hadn't have just emptied I'd be rock hard by that one action.

"You taste so good." She practically purrs.

"You like Daddy's cum?"

She nods sitting up. "I like it on me, over me, but most of all I like it in my mouth."

I grab her face pulling her up to me. "Careful Eden, I might take that as invitation."

"It is."

"You want me to cum in your mouth again?"

"I want you fill me up. I want to choke on it, drown on it."

"Fuck." I groan, pulling her up to her feet and then into my chest. I can feel it on me now. It's cool, sticky, all the warmth is gone.

"Promise you won't hurt me." She says quietly and I look down meeting those angelic eyes of hers.

"I won't Eden. I promise. I'll take care of you."

"Forever?" She says.

"For as long as you want me."

She nods. I can tell it's not quite the answer she wants. That she wants a declaration of my devotion but I won't give it. I'm not stupid, I'm not going to fool myself that what we have will last forever because deep down shit like that doesn't happen. Women like Eden don't end up with men like me. Or at least if they do, there isn't such an age gap. Because in the end, no matter how great this is, she will tire of me, she will grow out of me and I refuse to hold her down.

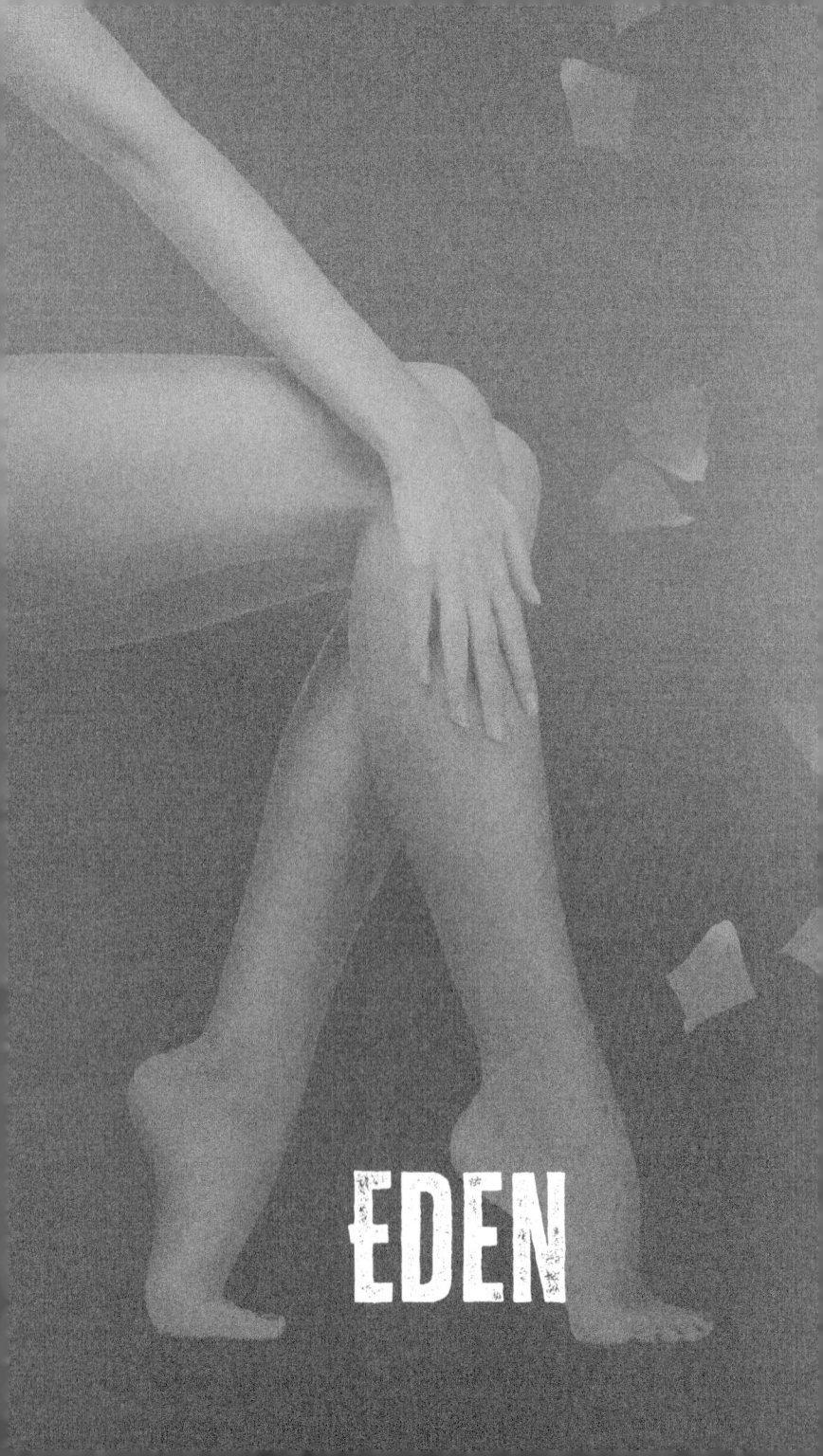

EDEN

Seventeen

I'm sat in a lecture, trying to pay attention. Only the professor is droning on about death of the author or some such philosophical shit that I'm not in the right headspace to understand.

My phone flashes and I pick it up reading the message from Katie and surreptitiously write back a reply.

"Miss Mathers?" The professor says and my stomach drops like I've been plunged into an ice bath. "Something more important than this lecture?"

"Sorry, I, my dog's sick." I say dropping my phone back and trying not to laugh at the worst excuse I just came up with.

He grunts like he doesn't believe me and to be fair I can't really blame him. And then he begins droning on again as I internally try not to fall asleep.

It doesn't help that they put him at 5pm. The last slot of the day. I personally think they do it on purpose. That it's a power play to torture us all.

When he's finally done and given back our assignments we all spring up, more than eager to get the fuck out.

"Miss Mathers." He calls. Fuck I'm definitely in more shit.

"Sir?" I say walking down slowly as all the lucky buggers around me get their freedom.

"Is there something going on that I need to be aware of?"

"In what way?" I ask.

"You're more distracted. Your grades are slipping."

I wince. I'm a perfectionist at heart, a workaholic too. To be told that I'm failing right now… I don't even know how to articulate my feelings.

"You're still passing Miss Mathers but this isn't you. You're normally top of the class."

"I…." I sigh. I don't even have an excuse.

"Look, if there's something going on, we can help, if you need someone to talk to."

"It's okay. It's just a blip." I say.

He gives me a look like he doesn't believe a word of it.

"Alright, well if you change your mind, my door is always open, as are any of the faculty."

I nod. "Thanks sir." And leave.

Katie is at the café, arms crossed, obviously annoyed that I've kept her waiting.

"Sorry." I say sitting down.

"You're twenty minutes late." She states pushing the fruit cooler at me.

"I got held up. My professor wanted a word after the lecture." I reply.

"About what?" She asks.

I wince. "Apparently I'm failing."

"What?" She gasps so loud a few people around us start staring.

"Not failing exactly, just, my grades are slipping. Apparently I'm not as attentive as I should be." I state.

"Is there something up?" She asks.

"No. I just…" I trail off. "I'm just overworked that's all."

"Maybe you should quit your job." She says and I pull a face.

"I'm not quitting."

"Eden, stacking shelves is not going to get you anywhere long term and besides Dominic gives you enough money. You don't even need to work."

"Yes I do." I snap back. I'm not just going to live off my stepdad's cash, and especially not now we're whatever the hell we are.

"I don't mean this to sound harsh but this whole 'I can stand on my own two feet' is bollocks. You've already done it long enough. You've made your point. Surely your degree is worth more than your pride?"

I scowl. I know deep down she's sort of right but that doesn't make it palatable. And besides, if I quit it will make things feel weird, make things be weird for me, in my own head, becoming totally dependent on Dominic.

"What does your mum think?"

I let out a laugh. "I'm not talking to her about it."

"Yeah I wouldn't if I were you." She says. Katie was the one who made me realise that I wasn't the issue, that my mother was. She was the first to call her a bitch, the first to tell me I'm not a waste of space, to tell me that a parent shouldn't be like that.

I guess I owe her a lot because at my lowest points she's been there, picking me up, letting my hide out.

I half want to tell her about Dominic but I don't know how to define it, how to explain it and my gut tells me she won't support it. That she'll say I'm an idiot, that he's taking advantage, and she won't stop going on until we stop. Right now I don't want any more drama.

So I keep my mouth shut.

"Where's Max?" I ask.

"At practice." She says. He's almost always at cricket practice. He's been in talks with scouts about going professional and he's putting in the hours to make sure he doesn't mess it up.

"I better head home." I say. We're meant to be having a family dinner though I doubt my mum will actually turn up.

"We're planning a camping trip, me, Max, Darla, Imogen, and Aron…." She says grinning.

"Me and Aron are breaking up." I state.

"Does he know that?" She asks.

"He does when I next see him." I mutter.

"Fine, then he's not invited, but say you'll come?"

"Yeah, if I'm free." I say grabbing my bag. "Let me know when."

GOOD GIRL

If I get back soon it might be me and Dominic for a little while and the thought of just spending a little time alone is enough to make me want to speed through every red light.

DOMINIC

Eighteen

"Are you fucking serious?" Eric growls.

I wince. I should have kept my mouth shut. Why didn't I keep my mouth shut? Fuck I'm an idiot.

"You're fucking her?" He half spits.

"No. We've not had sex."

"Dominic, she's your stepdaughter."

"I know." I snap.

"And you're fucking her?"

"WE. HAVEN'T. HAD. SEX." I state.

"But what, she's sucked your cock, you've done enough don't you think?" He says.

Jesus. I run my hand down my face. In what fucked up world did I even think I could explain this in a way that makes it not sound as perverted as it is?

"She's twenty one. She's not a child." I mutter.

"Yeah but you've helped raise her. She's as good as your kid."

"Fuck." I growl, slamming my fist on the desk. "Don't you think I don't know that? Don't you think I don't get how wrong this is?"

"So why are you still doing it?"

"I…" Because she's an addiction. She's an obsession. She's got inside my head, she's made me feel wanted, alive even. I haven't felt this way in years.

Only I can't say that. I can't admit out loud how far I've already fallen.

How far I've already sinned.

"You have to end this." He says. "You have to be very fucking careful how you end it because if Eden tells anyone… Jesus, Terri will have your balls for this."

"No she won't, she doesn't give a fuck about Eden." I say admitting what I've known for a while now. The woman isn't a mother to her, she barely wants to acknowledge she's her daughter. She'll only be pissed that it was me, her husband. That's where the anger will be.

"If this gets out, if people know, you'll be ruined."

"I know." I say.

"Dom mate, you have to be really careful here."

"I have to end this." I state.

"You do."

The problem is what I have to do and what I'm going to do are two entirely different things, even in this moment I know it. I won't end it. I can't end it.

I sink back in my chair. When I blink I can see her, sprawled on the table, covered in my cum. I see the way she's writhing in it, loving it.

My Lolita. Mine.

Fuck.

"I've had issues with our accounts." I say changing the subject. Getting to the real reason I wanted to see him. As my brother he's an equal partner. It's our names that are always emblazoned in lights. The Mathers Brothers. Entrepreneurs. Self-made men. Big time boys. "The auditors have found some irregularities."

"What irregularities?" He asks.

"Only a missing $250,000." I state meeting his eyes though how I can after what I've just confessed I have no idea.

"What?"

"Timothy is taking the lead internally but I've reached out to Bob Aldross at Scotland Yard."

"The cops?" He says.

"Someone is stealing from us, embezzling. I don't know who it is, but I know it's not me."

"It's not me either." He says like I'd suspect him. Like he'd ever be capable of it.

"I know mate." I say. "But we're going to do everything by the book, we'll find out who it is and the business will continue."

He nods. "Well keep me updated." He says. "About both these issues."

I grunt in reply. He's going to hound me now. He's going to keep checking until I confirm I've done it.

I get up and pour another coffee. We're meant to be having a family meal tonight. It was my idea that we start this, that we spend one dedicated night a week as a family. Only the Dominic who came up with that suggestion had no idea he'd be fucking around with his stepdaughter only a few months later.

And now Terri's raised it. As if she wants to play happy families all of a sudden.

And by god is this going to be awkward.

EDEN

Nineteen

Before I even get to the gates I see his flashy sports car parked up by the side of the road. He's sat leaning against the bonnet, scowling.

"Why are you here?" I say getting out and walking towards him.

"You won't respond to my messages, you won't pick up my calls. I figured if I started stalking you sooner or later you'd break."

"I've been busy."

He scoffs. "Doing what?"

"I have work, and my degree assignments." I state.

"No you don't."

"Excuse me?"

"You're doing English Lit. It's a doss degree. Anyone could do it. And your job is stacking shelves. Hardly taxing stuff." He says.

"Fuck you." I snap.

"No Eden. Stop pretending to be bigger than you are, more important than you are. You're lucky I even bother to spend any of my time on you at all."

I laugh shaking my head and as I do I spot a flash of red.

Shit. Dominic's car. He's driving home. He's…

He looks at me as his car slows. I can see he's pissed. He makes a point of shaking his head just a little and then the gates open and he drives in as if I'm not here. As if I don't exist.

"You know what Aron, you're right, you should spend your time on bigger things, better things."

He smirks.

"Why don't you go find some other girl who's got nothing going on in her life? Because you and me, we're over."

He goes to grab me and I jump aside before getting into my car and as I drive through the gates I can see him, still stood, glaring at me in my rear-view mirror.

The house feels empty when I get in. I know Dominic is here but it feels so cold, so off.

I dump my bag, kick off my shoes and storm into the kitchen half expecting him to be making a coffee. But he's not there.

He's not in the main living room either, or the snug.

I walk to his office and tap lightly on the shut door.

"Come in." He says and I can hear it, the tone, the more than obvious hint to his voice.

"Hi." I say stepping inside.

"Hi." He says glancing up then looking back at whatever paperwork he's pretending to focus on.

"How was your day?"

He sighs. "Long."

"Want a coffee?"

He grunts.

I'll take that as a yes then. I walk over to the coffee machine and start making it the way he likes. I can feel his eyes on me. I can feel him watching me but as I turn back, mug in hand, he's staring at the paper again.

"Here you go." I say putting it on his desk and stepping back.

I just want him to look at me. I just want some sort of acknowledgement. And then his eyes snap to me and I change my mind. I can see the anger, the jealousy, the streak of something undefinable.

"You're still seeing him?" He says narrowing his eyes. As if we're in a real relationship. As if he's not still married to my mother.

"We just broke up." I say.

He lets out a puff of air like he doesn't quite believe me. "How come?"

"Because I wouldn't have sex with him." I say meeting his look head on.

"He broke up with you because you wouldn't fuck him?" He growls and I hear it the protectiveness now. Is it sad that tone gives me hope?

"I broke up with him." I reply moving to lean against the desk.

"Why not?" He asks.

"Why not what?" I ask.

"Have sex with him?"

I let out a low sigh. Here we go. "I'm a virgin."

"Excuse me?"

"I'm a virgin." I repeat it looking back up at him.

He looks like he doesn't believe me. He looks like he thinks I'm lying.

"What you think because I've sucked your dick and you've finger fucked me a few times that I'm some kind of whore?" I snarl.

"No that's not what I think." He says moving to hold my waist. "I just…" He shakes his head. "The way you act, the way you are, you've had boyfriends Eden."

"Yeah well maybe I don't want to sleep with them."

"Are you saving yourself?" He asks and I scoff. Now he's making me sound like some kind of saint and we both know I'm not that either.

"No I just don't want to fuck them. I…" I trail off. This is not how I was planning this evening to go.

"You what?"

"I want to fuck you." I say. "I want you to be my first."

"Eden…" He says and I hear the warning there, but I hear the want too.

"Would you do it?" I ask.

He shakes his head. "You're my kid. This is wrong. All of this is wrong."

"No it's not." I say putting my hands on his chest and he pulls me closer so that I'm practically straddling him. "We're not even related. Not really. We're two consenting adults. You want me and I want you so what's the problem?"

"Because I raised you. I took you to school, took you afterschool clubs, to your prom…"

"And now I want you to take my virginity." I say taking his hand putting it under my skirt.

He shakes his head but he's pulling my panties aside anyway. Plunging his fingers into me, sliding them so deliciously and I let out a moan.

"This is wrong." He says as he starts curling away, teasing that spot inside me that makes me mewl so loudly for him.

"So wrong." I agree as I start gyrating, encouraging him more.

"You're my kid." He murmurs moving his hand faster, bring me closer and closer to my climax.

"Please Daddy. Please." I moan.

He grabs my face, plunges his tongue into my mouth as I come apart and I scream, I writhe, I pour out my release as he steals each new breath from me.

And then I fall back panting on top of him as his fingers stay where they are buried in my pussy, submerged right to my core, right where they belong.

"I'll do it." He says. "Of course I'll do it."

I look up at him. "Promise?"

"How can I refuse you sweetheart?"

I grin. Fuck I've wanted this for so long now, wanted him. And now we're crossing this final line together. United in our damnation.

"But I'm doing it my way." He says. "On my terms."

"However you want me." I say back.

He pulls me back running his eyes over me like he's going to devour me right now. His fingers are still in me and by god can I feel myself still clenching around him.

"I'm going to take every bit of you Eden. I'm going claim every part of you."

"Do it." I say back. I'm ready. More than ready. I want him so much it hurts.

We both hear her call out. It rings out down the hallway.

Mum's back.

I jump off him and he wipes his fingers clean on his pants.

"Get under the desk." He says.

"What?"

He grabs me, shoving me down and I only just manage to crawl myself up into the hollow space before I hear the door open.

"Hi honey." She says.

"Hey." He replies. "How was your day?"

"Long. We've had to slash our project's timeframe in half. I'm going to have to put in some serious hours over the next month."

"Aren't you doing that already?" He says obviously concerned.

"Not really. I mean. I am Dom, but I can hardly say no, what with the redundancies and all."

"It's not a criticism." Dominic says.

"Good."

"I was thinking of ordering take away for dinner." Dominic says leaning back in his chair.

"You know I can't stand that stuff. It's so unhealthy." She moans.

"But Eden likes it, and besides we could all do with a cheat day every so often."

"I don't need cheat days Dom."

He sighs. "Fine, how about I make you a salad?"

"Fine." She says. "Where is she anyway?"

"Who?"

"Eden."

"Probably in her room. How am I meant to know?"

"Whatever." She mutters. "Let's do dinner early. I'm shattered and want to go to bed soon. I think I've got a migraine coming on."

"I'll finish this up then."

"Thanks." She says before I hear her click clack out the door.

And then I sit waiting until Dominic pulls me out. And god help me he's grinning.

"That was not funny." I say.

"Talk about a close call." He says. "Wait a moment then you'll be fine to go."

I nod. "So, take out for dinner huh?"

"Unless you'd prefer a salad too?" He smirks.

"No thanks." I say before half sauntering out.

DOMINIC

Twenty

I know I said I'd end it. I know that's what I agreed.

I know it's wrong. That this has to stop. She's my stepdaughter for fucksake. There's no way we can continue this, no way we can think we'll get away with this.

But the thought that she's a virgin, that she's never even been fucked before? Jesus. I groan. I'm making a god damn salad and I'm groaning.

She's a virgin. My little Lolita. My angelic minx.

And she wants me to fuck her, to be her first. I glance down and my cock is so hard right now. For fucksake.

I dump the leaves back in the colander and head up to my room. I'm going to need to by some seriously restrictive boxers from now on because there's no way I'm going to stop thinking of Eden naked, with her cunt weeping out after I've fucked her.

I can hear Terri in the shower and I make a quick move to change my boxers, and my trousers. I was technically still in my work clothes anyway so it shouldn't look that weird.

I pull on a pair of joggers. I'm not usually one for casual clothes but right now I need something that covers and with a large jumper, if we're all sat around I'll be able to conceal any hard on relatively easily enough.

Terri comes out the bathroom and gasps as she sees me.

"Didn't mean to make you jump." I say.

"It's okay." She replies. She's got a towel wrapped around her but I can see finger bruises on her arms, on her wrists too, as if someone's pinned her down. And recently.

I try not to stare but there's no reason for her to have such markings.

"When's dinner?" She says making a point of turning her back to me as if my looking at her is making her uncomfortable.

"I'm just doing the salad now. Shouldn't be more than half an hour at most."

"Perfect." She replies throwing me a look. She wants to dry herself I realise and she doesn't want me seeing her when she does it.

What's she hiding? I shake the thought. I'm being ridiculous.

"I'll see you downstairs." I murmur leaving her to it.

Eden is in the kitchen by the time I get down. She's prepping the tomatoes, the cucumber, all the salad so I don't have to.

"Thanks." I say grabbing a bottle of white.

She smiles. "Anything for you Daddy." She half whispers and I give her a look. Not with Terri in the house. We can't be reckless.

"Do you want a drink?" I ask.

"Yes please."

I pull the cork and pour out two glasses, passing one to her. She eyes it as if confused.

"You're letting me drink drink?"

"You're an adult. One glass can't hurt." I say. "And it's not like you don't drink when you're out."

"I don't actually. At least not all that often."

"So you are a good girl then?"

She smirks. Just as Terri walks in.

"Are you..?" She says and then she looks at me. "Are you letting her drink?"

"It's just a small glass Terri." I say pouring her out one. If she's lubricated she'll be happier. We'll all be happier.

She shakes her head taking it from me. "If you get her drunk..."

"She's an adult and anyway I don't think anyone can get drunk on that amount." I reply.

"Here's your salad mum." Eden says putting the bowl in front of her.

"Where's yours?" She asks looking more at me.

"It's still on its way. It should be here any minute." I say checking the app on my phone.

She grunts before digging in. "So I received a call from the college today."

Eden's eyes snap to her and I slightly narrow mine wondering where this is going.

"Apparently your grades are slipping?" Terri says almost smugly. Though I know I'm imagining it, no parent wants their child to do badly.

"I…" Eden says. "I've already spoken to them. They shouldn't have called you."

"It's a good thing they did because you wouldn't have said anything would you?"

Eden frowns. "I'm dealing with it."

"You better be. That college is not cheap. Dominic pays a lot of money to send you there, the least you can do is put some effort in."

"I am." Eden says.

"Terri stop." I cut across her. "Eden's been busting her ass of late. So her grades of dropped? No one is perfect all the time."

"That's not what you said the other day. You wouldn't shut up about how great Eden's doing." Terri snarls pointing her fork at me.

"Can we stop?" I murmur. I don't know where this is coming from but it's not helping right now.

"Maybe we should look at Edinburgh again. A change of scenery would do you good." Terri says.

"I don't want to." Eden says. "This is my home, my friends are here, everything is here. I'd have to retake the entire year if I transferred now."

"Then you need to buck up your ideas. Dominic is not here to fund your lifestyle."

"I don't think he is." Eden says dropping her head.

"Enough." I state. "Eden is doing what she can. And I'm more than happy to spend the money on her tuition."

Terri pulls a face and mutters something like 'waste of time' under her breath.

"Terri." I say.

"I'm going to go to bed. I've got a headache." She says getting up and walking away and by god have I never wanted her to go more. Whatever has gotten into her tonight is beyond me.

The doorbell pings and Eden gets up to go grab the food.

I watch as she comes back and lays it out. She's avoiding my gaze now. Like she's got something to feel ashamed about. We sit in silence for a few minutes while I eat and she more picks at hers.

"I'm not failing." She says.

"I don't think you are."

"I just." She screws her face up. "I've got a lot on."

"Is it me?" I don't see how it can be but I'll back the hell off if she needs me too.

"No." She says quickly. "It's not you. I'm just struggling with managing my coursework, my lectures and my job."

"What can I do to help?"

She shrugs and then a grin creeps across her face. "I think you're already doing enough."

"I know you don't want to hear it but you don't need to work. And the hours you'd get back from not working could help relieve the pressure."

She nods. "I don't want to quit. I like my job. And other people can manage."

"You don't have to prove anything Eden."

"Yes I do." She says looking up with such a look in her eye. "All everyone sees is a spoilt little rich girl. All they think is that I have it so easy. That everything is laid out on a plate for me. That I don't have to work for anything."

"I don't think that."

"I know you don't." She says.

"Then why do you care what anyone else says?"

She winces. "I don't know. I just do."

I sigh. "You've hardly eaten anything." I state.

She grins. "Are you concerned for my health now?"

"Maybe I just want to keep your energy levels up."

Her eyes widen. "Are you wanting to play more?"

I pause. It's a double edged question. Of course I want to play more. Hell, I never want to stop but Terri's in the house. I can't risk anything right now.

"We can't. Not now. Not here." I say.

Her face falls slightly and if I'm honest I like the fact she's disappointed because it shows how much she wants me. A man old enough to be her dad. The man who is her actual stepdad.

"Terri is going to be working longer hours." I say quietly. "So I was thinking…"

She's staring at me, biting her lip, I bet if I stuck my hand in her panties she'd be wet right now with the thought of where I'm going with this.

"…maybe we could go away."

"Where?"

"Just away. Where no one knows us. I could take you on an actual date."

"And then would you fuck me?"

The question makes my dick jerk. Makes my pulse race too. Christ do I want to do that. And she's right, I can hardly take her virginity while we're listening out for her mum the whole time.

"Yes Eden. I will fuck you."

She gets up. "Good." She murmurs. "But make it soon because this waiting is killing me."

"Where are you going?" I ask.

"You won't play right now but that doesn't mean I can't by myself." She says.

I frown barely registering the words before it sinks in what she's doing. Fuck. The little tease is pulling that stunt?

EDEN

Twenty-One

It's not my intention for him to follow.

It wasn't my intention to tell him what I was going to do either.

But talking about us, talking about going away, about him actually taking me on a date and then us having sex has pushed me beyond my limits, beyond my sanity.

I'm practically running to my room, stripping my clothes off, getting into the shower and grabbing the bullet vibrator.

I need to cum. I need to cum right now or I'll storm back through this house and fuck my stepdad irrespective of whether my mum can hear or not.

I lean against the tiles, groaning as the toy comes to life.

But barely seconds later and the door opens and Dominic is standing there. Sans clothes.

My eyes widen. He's going to risk this, now?

"Did you get too horny my little Lolita?" He says and I laugh at the reference. Perhaps I am a Lolita. My behaviour right now certainly seems to suggest it but as I stare at his engorged dick I don't really care.

"We're not having sex." I say.

"No." He agrees. "But I am going to make you cum." He grabs the toy from my hand. "Without the need to use this either."

I smirk as he switches it off and tosses it over to land perfectly on a pile of towels.

He tilts his head stepping further under the water and it splatters onto his body in a way that I can't help but run my hands over.

"You're so fucking hot." I say.

He grins kneeling down, putting his shoulders between my legs as just as I close my eyes, half drooling from the thought of what he's about to do he lifts me up, throwing my legs behind him and his mouth finds my pussy as he holds me upside down.

"Oh Jesus Christ." I gasp as I grip his legs so tightly. Locking my ankles together.

"Ssssh. You have to be quiet."

"I hate being quiet." I sigh.

"And I hate it too." He says before he starts sucking, rolling my clit, making me struggle not to start moaning but it escapes me anyway.

He gives me a look before grabbing a flannel and shoving it in my mouth.

"If you can't behave you have to suffer the consequences." He says before he begins devouring me again.

I moan then. I moan so loudly and thank god the fabric swallows the majority of it.

His tongue is incredible as he licks and teases me. My pussy throbs and I clench one of my legs around his head, pulling him in, keeping him right where I need him.

"Oh fuck Dominic." I moan but he can't make out the words.

He's too busy eating at me anyway to care what I'm saying and I realise he loves giving oral as much as I do. God this man is perfect.

He swirls his tongue, he laps at me, I know I'm wet from more than just the shower water and he sucks it all up. I shudder as he does it and he turns his attention back to my clit. He flicks my bundle of nerves with his tongue over and over, teasing me to the point where I know I'm about to fall and then he slows down just a little before picking it up again.

I dig my hands into his thighs, I dig my nails in too. I'm half rabid with my need for release and he sucks my clit in over his teeth and rolls over and over and until my body is shaking and I can't take anymore.

"Oh fuck. Of fuck. Of fuck Dominic." I scream as something inside me breaks. As it feels like I'm pissing myself, as I flush out more than just my normal amount of cum all over his face. Only it keeps coming, on and on and I squirm desperate to stop it but I have no control.

He grunts pulling away and as he sets me back on my feet I know I'm bright red with embarrassment.

I pull the fabric from my mouth. Toss it on the floor. "I didn't mean…"

He frowns watching me as if he's amused by something.

"I think I just pissed myself." I say feeling for the first time ever like the inexperienced girl that I am around him.

He lets out a laugh. "That wasn't pee Eden."

"What…?"

"You don't know what you just did, do you sweetheart?"

I shake my head.

"You squirted." He says.

"What?"

"You just squirted Eden. And what's more you did it all over my face."

"That's, that's a good thing?" I ask.

He grins running his hands over his skin as if he wants whatever the hell liquid that left my body to soak into his very pores.

"It's the best. The fucking best."

I gulp as the realisation sets in that maybe I'm not such a freak after all.

"And now that I know how to make you do it, I'm going to keep on. I'm going make you squirt so many times. Make you squirt all over Daddy."

I grin but I still feel uncomfortable and yet he's so turned on right now. He's loving it so much.

I step closer to him before dropping to my knees. "In that case, can your Lolita have her reward please?"

His eyes say it all as I take hold of him. And as I start to lick slowly from the very base of his dick he shuts his eyes, twisting his hands in my hair.

DOMINIC

Twenty-Two

She's on her knees, staring up at me with those big brown beautiful eyes. And she's licking my cock as she does it.

My Lolita. She called herself that.

My perfect fucking angel.

This is not how this evening was meant to end. I had it all planned out, an awkward dinner, an awkward conversation. In my head I was going to do it, to call it off. As I drove back I reiterated it over and over to myself.

About what I was doing. About what I was risking. About how much I would lose if this ever got out.

And then I saw her with that boy. Fuck, just seeing them together made me so mad that when we were alone I needed to reclaim her, needed to prove to her that I alone can touch her in ways no one else can. And I needed to prove to myself that she wanted me more than anyone else too.

So now we're here, with her mouth caressing my cock and her hands fondling my balls as I enjoy every minute.

My Lolita.

I am going to fuck her.

As she slides me into her mouth that's the thought that rings out most in my head. That soon this cock will be sliding into that tight needy little cunt of hers, entering into the very depths of paradise itself and as she starts to suck on me all I can think is how her muscles will suck and clench with each hard thrust I make.

"Eden." I groan.

She pulls off with a pop. "Are you enjoying this Daddy?"

"Very much so." I say. How the hell could I not be?

She literally squirted on me less than five minutes ago. I can still feel it, sticking to my eyelashes, to my lips, to my stubble. And the taste, Jesus the taste of her.

She's the most incredible mix I've ever had. Her cum is the finest delicacy, the purest aphrodisiac known to man.

I groan again, grabbing her hair, taking charge.

She moans in response, letting me move her head, letting me control her movements as I thrust into her.

I'm hitting the back of her throat, sliding down it. Her makeup is streaming everywhere. Black streaks of mascara run down her face but in this moment she's never looked more beautiful.

"I'm going to fuck you Eden." I say. "I'm going to fuck you so hard."

She moans, trying to swirl her tongue but I'm moving her head too quickly now. I want to cum, I want to spurt down her throat and fill her up with it.

She shuts her eyes, screws her face up but I know she's still loving it. This girl loves sucking cock and it's my cock she wants the most.

"Suck your Daddy." I say. "Suck him good."

She moans more. Yeah this is turning her on. The little minx likes being told what to do, likes being dominated.

"When I cum you swallow it all down. Don't you dare spill a drop." I say.

She nods as best she can but I barely allow the movement because I'm hurtling towards my release and right now I am being selfish. I've made her cum for fucksake, now it's my turn.

She moans as I slam into her throat one final time and then I cum so hard not caring if Terri does hear.

She pulls off swallowing quickly and I grab her head.

"Lick me clean. Lick it all up."

She grins. "Yes Daddy." She says moving to follow my instructions and I lay back against the tiles, letting me breath calm, feeling my cock slowly go flaccid and enjoying the delicious sways of a nineteen year old's devotion as she licks over and over.

EDEN

Twenty-Three

We're going away. Dominic suggested it and now we're actually doing it.

He says he's sorted everything. He's picked a hotel. It's a few hours' drive away. And tomorrow I'll be sat beside him as we drive away on an actual date. A weekend of dates. A getaway.

I can't get my head around it. I can't quite believe it.

I spent the day shopping for underwear and new clothes. I want to look incredible, I want him to want me more than ever.

And most of all I want to make sure that he doesn't change his mind. That he doesn't back out. That he fucks me.

When I get home I see my mums car in the drive. She's been working so much of late I'm more surprised when she is home than when she isn't. Not that I'm complaining because her being away gives me plenty of alone time with Dominic.

I unlock the door and carry my bags up to my room. I don't want her to spot them, not that she'll know who they're for but the fact that I'm buying underwear, expensive underwear at that, is something I'd rather keep from a woman who delights in picking every aspect of my life to pieces.

When I'm done hiding them I go back downstairs. Dominic will be home soon and it's my turn to cook anyway.

Only she's in the kitchen. Back to me, leaning against the counter.

I go to leave but her tone makes me pause. Makes me hesitate.

"…Of course Colin." She purrs. "No, I'll be there."

The man on the line says something and she laughs. Flirtatiously. "I wouldn't dream of it. If you're going I'm going and besides we can sneak off early, just like always."

The man says something else and she laughs more. "Oh I'll be sure too. I'll buy some especially, black lace, just how you like."

I pull a face not wanting to hear anymore but I can't exactly walk anywhere because my shoes on the marble would give away that I'm here. I mean how she hasn't already picked up on it I don't know.

She hangs up, sighing like some sort of lovesick teenager. Confirming everything I've heard. Everything I now know.

She's having an affair. She's cheating on Dominic.

"Who was that?" I ask.

She turns staring at me, her face going so pale. "Just Dominic."

"No it wasn't."

"Eden…"

"You said Colin. So how about you stop lying and tell me who it was." I say

She pulls a face. She knows she's fucked up. I can see it in her eyes. "My boss if you must know."

"Your boss?" I snap and then I put it together. "You're fucking your boss?"

"Don't use that language." She says.

"Why, it's true isn't it?" I reply.

"It's not like that. You don't understand." She says so dismissively.

"Yeah you're right I don't. You're having an affair, you're cheating on Dominic."

"Like he isn't seeing other people." She retorts and I try so hard not to flush.

"Do you know that for a fact?" I ask.

"No." She mumbles as she sits down and I realise she's drunk. Again. "He probably isn't. He's too good for that. Too noble."

"You're right he's too good." I snap.

"Stop judging me. Stop seeing him as the hero all the time. He's not even your real father." She shouts. She's angry now, defensive. Reverting back to the abusive parent trick to get me to obey. "I have a right to be happy, to feel wanted." She says slamming her hand into the quartz.

"And Dominic doesn't make you feel like that?"

"What is this marriage counselling?" She scoffs. "No he doesn't. Sure he wants sex, sure he tries but he doesn't do it for me. Not anymore."

"And your boss does?"

"Yes he does actually."

"So why don't you leave Dominic? Start afresh? Hook up with your boss?"

"How can I? Dominic has all the money. This house, my car, even your tuition was paid by him. You're half of the reason I'm trapped here because no other man would take you on."

I screw my face up. No wonder she resents me if that's how she sees it. But she has a good job, a well-paid job, god knows what's she's doing with her salary because Dominic makes sure she doesn't need to spend a penny on anything.

"So you're using him as a cash cow?" God she makes me sick.

"He's happy enough." She says almost dismissively. "He gets to keep up the pretence of a good marriage which ensure his investors pay out and his business is successful."

"That's your definition of happiness is it?"

"Don't act like he's the one being wronged here. I cook his meals, I make sure his home is clean, presentable..."

I shake my head. She rarely cooks and we have a cleaner twice a week. She's delusional if she thinks she contributes anything meaningful to this house.

"...I listen to him when he tells me about his day no matter how boring it is, no matter how much I don't give a fuck." She continues.

"He deserves more than that." I state.

"Does he?" She says.

"Yeah he does. He deserves to be with someone who actually cares for him, who actually loves him, who isn't just using him. He deserves to be loved too."

Her eyes dart behind us and I know he's there even before I turn.

"What's going on?" He asks so calmly.

"Nothing." Mum says quickly.

"Eden?"

I shake my head. I don't think he's heard enough to know judging by his reaction right now and I sure as hell am not going to tell him.

"I have to go. I've got work to finish." I say not that it's true but right now I can't face him, I feel too guilty.

Guilty that my mother is having an affair, guilty that she's essentially been using him, and guilty about what we've been doing too. Afterall are we any better than she is?

DOMINIC

Twenty-Four

I obviously walked in on something. I just don't know what.

And now we're all sat around the table eating the pasta that Eden made not saying a word.

"This is delicious." I say and she gives me a small smile before dropping her gaze. Like she knows something I don't. Like she can't bear to look me in the face me now.

"It's good isn't it Terri?" I say to my wife and she nods ever so slightly before taking a mouthful of her wine.

"Alright, enough." I say. "Does someone want to tell me what the fuck is going on?"

"Language." Terri says like that's the most pressing issue.

I throw her a look only she's too busy glaring at Eden to notice.

"We were just talking about her studies." Terri says. "And about Edinburgh."

I see Eden tense and then she looks right back at her. "You seriously want to try that shit now?"

"Eden." Terri snaps.

"Terri." I growl and she looks at me. "Eden is not going to Edinburgh or wherever the fuck else you want to send her."

"But we decided…"

"No we didn't. You decided. It was your idea. Eden doesn't want to go and there's no way I'm going to force her."

Terri lets out a low breath. "Fine. If that's what you want." She says before looking back at Eden. "But don't forget what he does for you. Don't forget the sacrifices we both make for you. We've given you everything you could ever want. And without us, you'd have nothing, you'd be out on the streets."

Eden's hanging her head so low. Like she's half broken. Like her mother is intentionally trying to destroy her. I slam my fist down before I even realise I've even clenched it.

"Don't you dare say shit like that." I snarl.

"It's true. She needs to understand how this world works." Terri says.

"I think I understand just fine thank you." Eden mutters.

"No you don't. You don't have a fucking clue." Terri hisses.

"Enough. I'm done with this conversation. Why don't you go to bed? You've got a busy few weeks ahead." I say to my wife and she lets out a low rattling breath.

"Fine." She mutters getting up and walking away but not before throwing another look at Eden.

As soon as she's gone I reach out to her with my hand only she flinches.

"What was that about?" I ask.

She shakes her head. "It's been a long day."

"You know you can tell me anything right?"

She nods looking at me. "I think I'm going to go to bed too. I've got a headache."

I frown as she goes. There's some serious shit going on and I don't understand it.

So I sit, eating the rest of my dinner by myself and then I get up and clear everything away. Terri is leaving tomorrow. One of her suitcases is already packed by the front door. She's going to be on the road for a fortnight.

I don't understand how any job can demand such hours but she laid out her itinerary, detailing all the places they were going too while working this project, as if she thinks I don't believe her. And to be perfectly honest I'm more excited by her absence than I should be.

Because Eden and I will have a whole two weeks to ourselves. And after this weekend I know exactly what we're going to get up too.

As I turn off the lights I look around my home and make a mental note of all the places I'm going to fuck Eden. I want to be able to walk into every room in the house and know that I've had her sprawled, naked, leaking out my cum from at least one, if not all, her orifices.

Just the thought makes me hard, and I tuck my erection into my belt. Hopefully Terri is fast asleep by now so it won't make much difference.

In fact I'm half tempted to sleep in the spare room. Partly because she'll no doubt be snoring and partly because I'm so pissed at how she just treated Eden I'm not sure I can stand to even be in the same room as her.

But when I open the door I see her lamp is on.

She looks up at me and smiles. "You took your time."

"I didn't realise you were waiting up." I say. "I thought you'd be asleep by now."

She smiles climbing out of bed. She's wearing one of her silk nighties that cling to her body and I can see her nipples poking through.

"I thought perhaps we should kiss and make up. Seeing as we won't be able to for a while." She says putting her hands on my shirt, slowly unbuttoning it.

"Are you..?" I pause. "Are you wanting to have sex?"

She never wants too. She never initiates it. What the fuck is going on right now?

"Is it wrong for a wife to want her husband?" She says putting her hand on my cock and then grinning as she feels how hard I am. Only I'm not hard for her. I'm hard for Eden.

"Someone is more than ready." She says stepping back dropping the straps from her shoulders and exposing herself for me to look.

And I can't help it I do. My eyes stare at her, but not in want, not in desire. I'm examining her. My wife. Sick as I am, I'm comparing her to the girl I want, who's no doubt tucked up in bed at this very moment just down the hall.

"Fuck me Dominic." She says. "Fuck your wife."

I narrow my eyes. Fuck it'd be so easy too. To sink my cock into her and all the while think of her daughter's cunt but I can't do it. I won't do it. Maybe I'm too principled now. Strange fucking principles I have anyway to somehow justify messing with my own stepdaughter while refusing to touch the woman I'm legally wed to.

"I'm not in the mood." I say.

She laughs. "That's not true. You're a man. You're always in the mood. And besides I can feel little Dom is ready for me."

I shake my head. "I've got a headache." I say. "I'll sleep in the spare room. You've got a big day tomorrow so I don't want to keep you up."

And then I get the hell out before she can say anything more. Before she can do anything more. Before I have to look at her anymore either.

EDEN

Twenty-Five

She's gone. She left so early this morning I didn't even hear it and as selfish and self-centred as I am I couldn't be more happy. Because now Dominic and I have a whole fortnight.

Of just us. Alone.

Starting with a weekend away. And by this time tomorrow I plan to have fucked him so many times my pussy is sore from it.

I let out a little giggle. I know I should feel guilty. I know after all the revelations yesterday I should feel some reservations but I don't. If anything I feel better about what we're doing because of the fact my mum is having an affair.

Because she can hardly judge us when she's fucking her boss.

And then my eyes widen. She's away for two weeks with her boss. She's literally going to be cheating on Dominic as we cheat on her.

Damn that's fucked up. Even I know that.

But will it stop me? No.

Will I even reconsider this? Hell no.

For a second I consider telling Dominic but a voice in my head tells me not too. It's not my secret and besides, as much as my intentions would be good, I don't want him to think that I'm only saying it so that he'll leave her. I don't want him to think that of me. And for all the times my mother has called me manipulative I feel like that's what it would be, manipulation, using this to get what I want when in reality I want Dominic to choose me for me alone, not because of what my mother has done, not because of her at all.

I take my time doing my hair, doing my makeup, putting on the dark blue silk and lace set I bought that hoiks my breasts up and makes them looks so good. And then I put on a summer dress. A new dress. It scoops low enough to make your eyes drop to my cleavage without being overtly slutty. It's subtle slutty. Classy slutty. Not slutty slutty.

I head down the stairs as quickly as I can. I can hear the radio blasting so I know Dominic is already up and about.

He turns when he sees me and looks me up and down. Obviously checking me out.

"Good morning." He says smiling.

"Good morning." I grin back.

"How's the headache?" He asks.

"All better." I say pulling a bar stool out and sitting on it.

"Is that so?" He murmurs plating up another pancake onto the pile he's making in the centre of the island.

"I love pancakes." I say and then curse myself for sounding like an excitable child and not a grown woman.

"I know." He replies. "That's why I made them."

I smile up at him and he tells me to dig in which obviously I do. After wolfing down half the pile though I realise he's not eating.

"I was thinking of something else for breakfast." He says when I question him.

"Like what?"

He grins. Fuck me. Is he really?

"I thought we could start this weekend off properly." He says. "That is once you're done eating."

"I'm done." I say putting my plate out the way.

He laughs. "I thought you loved pancakes?"

"I do. But I think I'll love what you've got planned more."

"Hmmm." He says picking me up and laying me over the island on my back, narrowly missing the condiments he's laid out. "Shall we test that theory?"

"Yes please." I say as he pulls my dress up and slips my panties off.

"Got to have a good serving of cream." He says smearing some down me as I gasp. "And a dash of honey too."

He squeezes it out, literally from the bottle.

"Jesus."

He looks up. "Breakfast is served." He murmurs before lowering his mouth as he spreads my legs so wide I practically do the splits.

I moan as he drags his tongue over me. Lapping away. Licking it all off.

"Fuck yes." He says lifting his face and I can see the cream caught on his stubble. "Keep those legs there." He says moving his hands so that one is parting my lips even more and the other is teasing my clit.

"Dominic." I moan as he licks and sucks me more. "That feels so good."

"Yeah?" He says.

I try to keep so still. I locked my ankles around the edge of the island as best I can but it's hard to focus on anything other than what this man is doing to my body.

"Your cunt is so delicious." He groans before sliding his fingers in. "So fucking perfect but by the time this weekend is out I'm going to make it so swollen and sore."

"I want you to do it." I gasp as he starts pumping inside me. "I want to be unable to walk from what you do to me."

"Oh don't worry about that." He says lowering his mouth again. "I'm going to fuck you so good you won't know what's hit you."

I shut my eyes losing myself in the salaciousness of his words and the ecstasy of his touch. I don't know how the hell I'm going to survive the weekend let alone a whole two weeks of this.

"Oh fuck, Jesus. Fuck." I gasp.

"Scream for me Eden." He says. "Scream for Daddy."

And god help me I do. I scream so loudly and it echoes in the empty house, echoes around us as it goes on and on, as long as he keeps me cuming.

And then he sits on the stool staring at my exposed pussy, at where I'm dripping out onto the counter, watching as I get my breath back.

"Now we're ready to go." He says.

I let out a giggle, half of exhaustion. It's not even ten o'clock and I know I'm going to need a lot more than just pancakes to keep up with this man.

DOMINIC

Twenty-Six

I pack the car up while she cleans herself up.

I didn't plan on making such a mess, but when the opportunity presented itself I figured what the hell, and besides I like the fact she's already cum for me. I'm planning on keeping track. I want to have a record of how many times I can make her orgasm before the fortnight is up. Hell, I might even get the number printed out and framed.

It'd make a nice private joke for the two of us. A nice reminder when we need it.

We drive out, with the sun shining and a grin right across her face. A grin I know I put there.

She's changed her dress. I guess I made too much of a mess with the old one. She's now wearing a deep red one that accentuates her skin tone so much she looks like she's glowing.

Once we're out of the city and away from any prying eyes I put my hand on her thigh. It's possessive, I know that, but the look she gives me when I do it tells me she likes it.

"I've booked a table at the restaurant tonight." I say. "But if you want we can eat in the suite."

"Suite?" She says.

I grin. "Only the best for my girl."

She laughs. "Is that so?"

"Do you doubt me?"

"Not for a minute." She says. "In fact I'm a little concerned by how much I trust you."

"In what respect?"

"Well, here we are disappearing off, with no one knowing where we're going. What if you had bad intentions?" She says. "What if you were planning on taking advantage of me?"

"Very logical concerns." I say moving my hand under her dress and she throws me a look like she was expecting me to just act like she's not wanting this right now. "But if I were to take advantage…" I begin, stroking her clit through her panties.

"Shit." She gasps and I chuckle.

"If I were to take advantage Eden." I say glancing at her as much as I can whilst ensuring we don't crash. "There wouldn't be much you could do to stop me, would there?"

She shakes her head. She's biting her lip again but she's also sinking back into the chair giving me a better angle to work with.

"My little Lolita wants to be taken advantage of I think." I say as her panties start to soak through.

"Maybe I do." She gasps.

"Then I guess you're lucky that I'm willing to play my part so well."

"So well." She moans.

"So the question is Eden, how well will you play your part?"

She shudders, she kicks out, her feet hit the side of the footwell in front of her and she reaches up, trying to brace herself as she falls apart for me.

And I can't help it, I laugh.

She's so fucking perfect and by god am I going to enjoy manipulating her body, using her body, showing her exactly why she wants me so much.

By the time we get to the hotel I've made her cum so many times she's drenched my leather seat. Not that I care. It's worth the expense just to hear her moans each and every time she falls over the edge.

She looks so flustered, yet so beautiful, as she gets out, flattening her dress, trying to be respectable when we can both smell her arousal.

The porter takes our bags and I take her hand leading her inside.

She stares around, looking at the grand entrance in amazement.

We get our keys from the concierge and I lead her to the elevator. I'm not in a hurry to get to our room but at the same time I'm still nervous on the off chance we might bump into someone we know.

"This place is incredible." She says as the doors ping shut.

"Wait till you see the suite." I reply. It's going to blow her mind.

We step out and again I take her hand. She looks down grinning and half squeezes mine like she likes me doing it so publicly.

The bags are already there waiting. A man shows us around and checks we're happy.

"Its fine thank you." I say.

"We hope you and your wife enjoy your stay Mr Mathers, if there's anything you need please let reception know." He says before leaving us to it.

"Your wife?" Eden says as soon as the door shuts.

I turn but she's clearly not offended because she's half laughing.

"I guess they saw our names and assumed we were married." I stated.

"Instead of stepfather and stepdaughter." She murmurs moving closer.

"Indeed." I say.

She kisses me, her lips meeting mine and her tongue slipping eagerly into my mouth and then she pulls away.

"I want to eat here. I don't want to leave this suite. I don't want either of us to leave until we have too. And I just want you to fuck me. Now please."

I let out a low breath. God I want her. I want her so much but I also don't want to rush this.

"Are you sure?"

"More than sure."

"Alright. Wait here a moment. Don't come until I call." I say and she bites her lips, trying so hard not to smile as I walk away.

EDEN

Twenty-Seven

I'm standing here, grinning like an idiot, waiting for Dominic to call me.

My pussy is throbbing so hard. I'm a sticky wet mess from how he half tortured me on the journey but now that we're here, I wouldn't have this any other way.

I hear a pop. He's opened champagne I think. I wonder if he's covered the bed in rose petals too.

Jesus I hope not. I don't want it to be romantic in a soppy, cliched way. I just want him and me. Able to do what we want. Able to completely and utterly enjoy ourselves for as long as we want without having to answer to anyone.

"Eden."

I feel a flutter as I hear him call and I quickly unzip my dress. Perhaps I should have thought to do it sooner but hell, it's too late now, and anyway I want him to see me, without the restriction of clothes, I want him to see the new underwear, the way my breasts are, I want him to want me.

I step out and cross through the main lounge to where the master bedroom is. He booked us the penthouse and the whole way round is one way glass so we have the most incredible view, not that I'll be focusing on it, because with Dominic naked, he'll have my sole attention.

I walk into the bedroom and he's there, completely naked, bottle of champagne in hand.

"I see you ditched some clothes too." He says.

I nod. "I didn't want them to get in the way."

"Or waste time?" He teases.

He hands me the bottle and I swig it. It bubbles in my throat but in this moment I want a little Dutch courage just to calm my nerves.

He's watching me, studying me.

"We don't have do anything…" He says but I cut across.

"I'm just nervous but I want to." I say. "I want you Dominic. I've never wanted anyone like I want you."

He takes the bottle, drinks a little then puts the bottle down before pulling me to stand between his thighs as he sits on the end of the bed.

"You're so beautiful." He says staring at me, studying me. "I don't think you realise how beautiful you are."

"And you're so beautiful too." I say back running my hands over his muscles, feeling the smoothness of his skin beneath the dark markings. "My silver fox."

He smirks. "We make a good couple then."

"Are we a couple?" I don't know why I ask it but I guess my mouth is running away from me.

He narrows his eyes. "In my head we are. In my head you are everything I've ever wanted, everything I'll ever want."

"And in reality?"

He sighs. "I can't give you any more than I am right now. But I promise you, when I can, when I'm able to, I will."

My eyes widen. That's the closest he's come to a commitment. In this moment I'll take that, I'll take whatever he's offering me.

"How about we focus on the now?" I say. "Focus on what we can have right now."

He nods and his eyes drop to my breasts. "Is this new?" He asks feeling along the lace of the bra.

I giggle. "As a matter of fact it is."

"For me?"

"I might have made a few purchases."

"I see." He says reaching around and unclipping it before I can react. "I think I prefer you without a bra."

"I can hardly walk around outside without one. It would be indecent."

"As indecent as we are?"

"Perhaps." I say.

He's touching me, cupping my breasts, massaging them. He's not the dominant, possessive daddy figure, right now he's something else.

He sucks one of my nipples into his mouth and I let out such a moan. It sounds carnal, feral. Maybe it's the fact I know where this is headed this time but all my senses feel alive. I feel alive. On fire.

"Dominic." I groan.

He grabs my other breast pulling it so he can suck on that nipple too.

I arch my back, I lose myself as he does it. And then he swings us around so that I'm lying on the bed on my back.

I look up at him as he runs his eyes over me before sliding my panties off.

His dick is so hard. I can see the precum. I can see the way the tip is so red. He's so fucking turned on right now and it's for me. His erection, his wants, all of it is about me.

He leans over and grabs a towel.

"What...?"

"You might bleed." He says placing it under me.

"Oh." I say. I thought that was a myth, Some bullshit men bragged about to make it sound like they had big dicks.

"This will hurt. At least to begin with." He says. "But I promise I'll go slow, until you want me to go faster."

I nod. I'm ready for him. I'm ready for his dick. I'm ready for the pain too if that's what it takes to have him inside me. To have him properly.

He pulls a condom and I shake my head.

"I'm on the pill." I say quickly.

"Really?"

"I sorted it weeks ago."

He grins. "So you'll let me cum inside you?"

"I want you to cum inside me." I say.

He groans tossing the condom but picking the lube up. "The wetter we are the less it will hurt you."

I nod, spreading my legs letting him pour some on me despite the fact that I feel pretty wet with my own arousal.

The cold liquid drips down and if anything it turns me on more.

He crawls over me. His body held up by his arms but I can feel the heat of him and I can feel the tip of his dick touching me.

"Eden." He says softly and he kisses me, his lips parting mine and I moan as his tongue wraps around, twists, gets lost in my mouth.

And as he does it he moves his hands and starts to push into me.

DOMINIC

Twenty-Eight

Fuck she's so tight. I'm barely in and she's already gripping my cock for dear life.

I hear her whimper. Even as I'm kissing her, as I'm trying to relax her. The first time is always shit for a girl, no matter how romantic everyone plays it up to be but if I'm careful I can make this as pain free as possible and from then on I'll fuck her how I really want.

I push further in. She's not telling me to stop and until she does I'm going to bury my cock as far as I can inside her.

It doesn't help though that I'm thick, girthy, and long too. Not the ideal cock someone wants for their first time.

She raises her hips, trying to adjust the angle. I'm only halfway now but she's not getting any looser.

"Ssssh." I murmur as I see her wince again. "Just a little more, then I promise it'll start to feel good."

"How much more?" She gasps.

I glance down. She's got a least three more inches to take but I won't tell her that. And I won't give her that. She doesn't need to have all of me in her right now anyway.

"I'm going to start thrusting." I say and she nods.

I slide out, it feels like her muscles pull as I do it but when I slide back in it feels less tight. She's relaxing. Albeit slowly.

"Dominic." She gasps.

"Yeah?"

"Just do it."

"What?"

"Fuck me, just start fucking me. I can take the pain. I can do it."

I pull a face. "Are you sure?"

She nods. "The sooner you're in me fully, the sooner you can make it feel good."

My lips curl. She's right.

"If you need me to stop though, you tell me."

"Okay."

I push into her then. Push all the way. She gasps but she swallows whatever pain she's feeling. And then slowly I pick up pace. Her body rocks beneath me, she lies there, letting me fuck her letting me shove my cock into her however I want as if she's waiting for the pleasure to hit.

I drop my thumb to her clit and she looks at me.

"Trust me." I say. If I can make her cum then she'll be all the better for it.

"Make it feel good." She says as I start to circle her.

"Don't worry." I murmur. "Daddy's going to make it all better."

She nods. Fuck I didn't want to do that, to turn to the whole daddy kink and yet here I am saying it while I'm literally taking her virginity.

I wanted this to be simpler, cleaner perhaps.

She's rocking her hips though, meeting my thrusts. She's stopped whimpering too.

"You like that?" I say.

"Yeah." She replies.

I grin. "Good girl. You take my cock so well."

"I want you to teach me how to take it better."

"Oh I will." I murmur. By the time this weekend is done Eden's going to be so well trained in how to ride my cock. She's going to be an expert in it.

I push harder onto her bundle of nerves, I've made her cum so many times in the car that I know she's over sensitive now and as she starts to flush I can feel her muscles clenching, gripping me.

I groan as she does it. God it feels so much better than I thought. Her tight, needy little cunt is eager for me now.

"Is that good?" She gasps.

"So good. You're so good." I say.

She moans. I can hear she's close and I'm so close too. She grabs the sheets, grips them between her hands. Her body clenches more, tightens around my cock to an impossible degree and then she kicks out screaming, throwing her head back.

"Cum Eden. Cum on my cock." I growl. It's taking all of my restraint not to cum myself but I want her to go first.

She pants as I start to thrust harder, as I start to lose myself.

"Dominic." She moans but I barely hear her. I'm so close now. So close to this moment I've been dreaming of, obsessing of. Her cunt is so tight, so greedy as it takes me thrust after thrust and as I start to pump into her it feels like she's gripping me, milking me of every drop.

I growl out, gripping her body, holding her tight to me. She wraps herself around me and as we collapse onto the bed she lays on her side staring at me with a look of pure amazement.

But when I pull out, she whimpers again.

"I'm sorry." I murmur. "I promise from now on it won't hurt so much."

"It's okay." She says. "It's a small price to pay for finally getting what I wanted."

I smirk. "So you're happy then?"

"More than happy." She replies twisting to lay her back on the sheets. "I just got fucked by Dominic Mathers. I just lost my virginity to Dominic Mathers."

"You gave your virginity to Dominic Mathers." I correct her.

"Is it a good present for you Daddy?" She says.

Jesus fucking Christ, if my balls hadn't just emptied in her I think I'd have a raging hard on again at those words.

"The best present." I say before sitting up, pulling her legs apart and she squeals slightly.

"And this is your reward." I state. "My cum dripping out of your weeping cunt." And by god is it weeping. She looks so perfect now. Her lips are swollen, her entire cunt is flushed and out of that tight little hole my seed is dribbling down, mixing with the tinge of her virginal blood.

She blinks. "Is it really dripping?"

"Can you not feel it?" I ask before grabbing my phone and taking a picture. Perhaps she's too swollen right now to feel it. Too sensitive too. "Here, look at yourself."

She takes the phone and stares. "That's…" She blushes. "Can I have a copy of this?"

"You want a copy?" I ask.

"I want a souvenir."

I smirk. My girl is so fucking perfect. "Have all the souvenirs you want." I say sending it to her phone.

And then I pull the towel out. There's a little smear of blood on it, admittedly more than I expected, but it doesn't matter.

"Do you want this too?" I ask her holding it up.

She shakes her head. "No. You can keep that. It's your souvenir."

Yeah it fucking is, I think, slinging it to where our suitcases are. And I damn well will keep it. I'll vacuum seal it up, lock it in the safe, preserve it as an everlasting memento.

My very own holy relic.

And proof of my damnation too.

EDEN

Twenty-Nine

We're sat in the hot tub.

I didn't pack a bikini so I'm wearing absolutely nothing and neither is Dominic. I wonder if this might be a theme for the entire weekend. That we spend it completely naked, ogling each other, enjoying the short lived freedom we have.

The water feels soothing, calming almost but my pussy is still throbbing and a part of me wants to find out if it's from the abuse it's sustained or the want of more.

Dominic pours more champagne into my glass and I smile and sip it. He doesn't seem concerned with my alcohol intake. He's treating me like a fully-fledged adult.

And then I remember that we've just fucked. Actually fucked. If he doesn't treat me like an adult after that he's either an arse or a pervert.

"What are you thinking?" He says.

"I'm trying to decide if you're a pervert." I say.

His eyebrows raise as I laugh.

"Do you think I am?"

"No." I admit. "But I do think you have an unhealthy obsession with your stepdaughter."

"How unhealthy?" He asks pulling me to him and I move to straddle him, putting the glass aside.

"Very unhealthy." I half whisper before kissing his neck.

He yanks my hair not hard but enough to make me gasp.

"Do you want my cock already Eden is that it?"

"And if I do?" I say. "You did promise that you'd train me Dominic. I don't want you to rest on your laurels."

He grins. "Oh my little Lolita wants another lesson does she?" He says grabbing his dick, running it along my pussy as he starts to tease.

"Oh." I moan.

I rub myself against him, he feels so good pushed up between my folds and he shuts his eyes clearly enjoying it too. His hands reach up and he starts circling my nipples.

"You've got the most amazing tits." He says.

"And you've got the most amazing cock." I say back.

He smirks. "Yeah? How about you ride that cock Eden, show it what you can do."

I bite my lip, positioning myself over him and slowly sink down on top. He groans as I wince slightly.

"Does it still hurt?"

I nod. "Just a little."

"Sit then, let your body adjust." He says, massaging my breasts as if he's more than content occupying his time with just them right now.

"What are your kinks?" I ask.

"What?"

"Everyone has kinks." I say.

He lets out a laugh. "Are you so experienced now?"

"Maybe." I shrug. "Clearly you've got a daddy kink."

He shakes his head. "No I don't. I only have that with you. It's something about you."

"Being your stepdaughter and all?" I tease.

He leans forward, sucking on my right breast and I moan. "What a stepdaughter." He says before sucking more. I moan and he lays back with a smug self-satisfied look on his face.

"What other kinks?" I ask.

"Why do you want to know?"

"I want to try them. All of them. Whatever would turn you on."

He tilts his head as he looks up at me. "Alright. But I need to know your kinks too."

"I don't have any."

"Sure you do. You were watching lesbian porn the first time you sucked my cock."

I grin. Yeah I was. "I like watching it. It turns me on. But I'm not bi or anything."

"So you don't fancy some girl on girl fun?"

"Not really. Why would you want me too?"

He pauses. "No. I won't corrupt you in that way."

"No?" I half laugh. His dick is throbbing inside me right now. I think he's more than corrupted me enough.

He pulls a face for a moment. "Are you ready to ride Daddy's cock yet?"

I meet his eyes, god I can see how much he wants me right now, how turned on he is.

"I'm ready Daddy." I say lifting my hips, shifting my legs a little and then coming back down.

We both groan. In unison.

Just as he bottoms out I roll my ass and come back up. Just like the pornos.

"Oh fuck yeah." Dominic mutters, grabbing my hips, holding my body as I start to properly get into a rhythm.

His cock slides in and out. He's so thick it feels like my body is suctioned to him, but it feels incredible all the same. He's hitting every sensitive part inside and as my body jives he seems torn before staring at where we're connected and my bouncing tits in front of his face.

"Is that good?" I ask even though I know it is, I can see from his face that it is.

"So fucking good." He says. "You ride my cock so well."

"You feel so good inside me Dominic."

He grins. "Your cunt is made for me. Made for my cock."

I nod before throwing my head back. I'm not sure how much more of this I can take. There's something building inside me, something coiling and as his grip tightens I start to moan more and more. I'm going to cum I realise. I'm going to cum purely on the feel of his cock.

"Such a good girl." Dominic groans and I hear he's close too.

"Cum with me." I gasp but it's too late. I'm already there, already riding the euphoria that Dominic is sending through my body.

He grunts, raising his hips, thrusting into me now as I slow down because I'm unable to focus on my body movements now.

"I'm cuming Eden. I'm fucking cuming too." He groans and I can feel it, his dick jerking inside me, his cum pouring inside me.

"I can feel it." I gasp. "I can feel you cuming."

"Milk my cock. Milk me dry." He says and though I don't know what that means I guess my body does because I can feel myself still clinging to him, my walls are clenched so tightly and as he falls back I stay where I am, sat on his dick, not wanting to get off.

DOMINIC

Thirty

We stay like this for what feels like hours. Every time we fuck we stay on top of each other and she doesn't get off. I swear she must be full to the brim by now. Her cunt must be so rammed with cum it will come flooding out when she does eventually move.

But I wouldn't have it any other way.

I fuck her one last time before dinner, I pin her down against the side of the hot tub. I'm aggressive, domineering, but she seems to get off on it because as I pound almost mercilessly into her she cums harder than ever.

My sweet Lolita. My beautiful stepdaughter.

I really am moulding her.

When we get out I do the gentlemanly thing and give her a few minutes privacy. She's quick to wrap a towel around herself but as she half runs to the shower I can see it, my cum dripping down her legs. And fuck what a sight.

She squeals when she realises I've seen and I can't help but laugh.

Our food arrives and we sit in bathrobes and eat. Eden eyes all the seafood with a hunger I know I've helped create and watch as she digs in.

Christ she's even beautiful when she eats.

"What?" She says looking at me and I shake my head slightly.

"Nothing."

She leans back in her chair, looking around, taking in the view and then I feel her eyes back on me.

"Thank you for this." She murmurs.

"For whisking you off so that I can have my wicked way with you?" I smirk.

She laughs. "Perhaps. But I meant that you didn't need to do this. We could have stayed at home, we could have, you know…" She pulls a suggestive face. "Fucked there."

"Yeah we could have." I reply. "But I wanted to do this. I wanted to show you how I would treat you if I could."

"So it'd be fine hotels and fancy food then?"

"And you bouncing on my cock at every opportunity." I state.

"Hmmm that sounds quite an ask." She says.

"Does it?"

"Well, if your cock is inside me then how can I suck on it as much as I want?"

My jaw drops and now it's her turn to laugh.

"Why don't you have a gag reflex?" I ask.

She hesitates and then sighs. "Will you judge me if I tell you the truth?"

"I don't think I'm in a position to judge anyone and I certainly won't judge you."

"It was a way to distract boys when they wanted to have sex." She states.

"What?"

"If I sucked them off then they wouldn't pester to fuck me and I guess I just trained myself to not have one."

"You could have just said no." I half growl. I'm not angry at her. I'm angry at the fact she felt that was her only option.

"True. I could have and I did a lot of the times. But I like it. I like the feel of it, the taste of it, the way…"

"Stop." I say and she does. "I don't think I want to hear about you sucking other cocks."

"If it makes you feel better I only want to suck yours from now on."

I narrow my eyes for a moment. I know my jealousy is unfounded, hypocritical even, but I can't help feeling it anyway. "Eden I don't want you with anyone else." I say before I can stop myself.

"I'm not. I haven't been. Not since we started this." She says so seriously.

"I know it's unreasonable." I state. "I know I'm being a jerk right now."

"You're not." She says. "If I could I'd ask you to leave her, but I know it's not my place."

I screw my face up for a second. "If I could I would." I admit. "I just need time. And I appreciate how cliché that sounds, how every man says that to his mistress but I mean it…"

"So I'm your mistress am I?" She says half grinning and I grin too.

"Yeah I guess you are."

"Do you still have sex with her?"

"No." I see her face visibly react. See her body react too. "And I won't. I won't be with anyone else except you."

She gets up walking around the table and sits on my lap. "It sounds like we're on the same page then."

"It does doesn't it?" I reply.

"How about you eat your dinner and then you can show your mistress how good you can fuck her?" She says.

I groan. God she's insatiable. I feel like I've opened pandora's box but I love it all the same.

"How about you put that lack of gag reflex to good use and suck Daddy while he eats?" I say and she grins like I've just offered her the world.

"Oh Daddy." She says getting off my lap and I move my chair back just a little so that she can fit between my legs and the table top.

She unfolds the robe and of course King Dom is raring to go. She glances up at me, I think she likes the fact that I watch her and she starts working her charm as I groan and hold her head with one hand and eat as best I can with the other.

EDEN

Thirty-One

By the time the weekend's done I'm almost sad to leave and then I remind myself that mum is gone.

For two weeks.

If we want to we can literally continue fucking until the day she gets back.

"What are you grinning about?" Dominic asks as the porter takes our bags down.

"Well, I was just thinking how we have the entire house to ourselves." I say as he takes my hand and we head down to the lobby.

"What are you thinking Eden?"

"Nothing much. Only that we should make the most of it while we can."

He nods. "I've already considered it. I've drawn up a schedule."

"What?"

"I don't want you to skip out on any of your lessons."

"Lessons?"

"My little Lolita wanted me to train her didn't she?" He says and I bite my lip.

"Yes Daddy." I reply leaning into him slightly. "Teach me everything you know."

He laughs. "Oh I will Eden. And you're going to love every second of it."

I can feel my pussy throbbing. In truth I'm so sore from how much we've fucked already but if he pulled my dress up right here and shoved his dick in, in front of everyone, I'd be crying tears of joy all the same.

"Dominic Mathers?" A man says and we both jump. Dominic's hand slips from mine and he turns.

"Carl." Dominic says. "How have you been?"

"Good thanks. How's you? How's business?"

"Good. All good."

The man looks at me. He must be about the same age as Dominic but the difference is startling, he's got a little pot belly, whispery hair, definitely not the hot older guy vibe.

"This must be your wife. It's a pleasure to meet you." He says holding his hand out.

"Er..." I say trying not to blush.

"This is my stepdaughter actually." Dominic says as I shake his hand and Carl has the tiniest micro expression of a frown.

"I see." He says.

"She's been helping me on a special project. Eden, this is Carl Anderson, he's an old friend."

"A very old friend." Carl says half laughing. "Well I won't keep you. You're obviously off somewhere."

"Back home." Dominic says.

"Well safe journey. It was nice to meet you Eden." He says glancing between us. "And we should have a catch up soon Dom, it's been far too long."

"Yeah it has." Dominic says. "I'll drop you a message."

We walk away without saying a word. In truth I'm worried this might have scared him off, made him reconsider this.

But as we get to where his car is waiting he starts laughing. "Fuck me that got my adrenaline going."

"Mine too." I say.

"Special project." He says. "The only project you've been on all weekend is my cock."

I laugh again. "Don't you down play my hard work. You gave me a task and I've been very dedicated."

"Yes you have." He says but his eyes still glance around as if he's expecting someone else to pop out of the woodwork.

"Shall we go home?"

"Yes. And then we can have a performance review I think."

I shake my head at the cheesiness of it but Christ are my panties wet anyway.

DOMINIC

Thirty-Two

Terri's been gone a week and I don't think my cock has had a rest since. My balls are working overtime. And between Eden's greedy cunt and her incredible mouth she's more than happy to take my cum in whatever orifice I deposit it in.

I sleep in her room, beside her. I've even put my toiletries in her bathroom and my clothes in her wardrobe because it seems stupid not too.

I wake up to her incredible mouth sucking me off and by god every man should experience coming round like that.

She grins up at me as I pull the covers back and then I see she's not only playing with me she's playing with herself too.

"Did someone wake up all needy?" I groan. She's such a morning person and I most definitely am not.

She nods pulling her lips off of me. "Really needy."

"And you decided it was appropriate to wake me too did you?"

She tilts her head. "Did you want a lay in, on a week day?"

I grab her and pull her side aways across me so that her bare ass is in the perfect position for my hand and I run it over her, admiring the fine curve of her cheeks.

"Are you going to spank me?" She says and I can hear it, how she wants me too.

"Yes." I say. "And you're going to count them as I do."

"Yes Daddy." She says just as my hand comes down.

"Ow. One Daddy."

I smile. She's so fucking beautiful. Even laid here, half sprawled with her hair all frizzy. "Such a naughty girl." I say hitting her again.

"Two Daddy." She gasps.

"Does it hurt?" I ask her.

"Yes."

"Do you want it to hurt more?"

"Yes, I want to have your hand print on my ass all day."

"Yeah you do." I say bringing my hand down again and this time even I hear the sting as it makes contact.

She hisses. "Three Daddy."

"I think that's enough." I state.

She starts to get up only I push her back down. "Where are you going Eden?" I say. "Don't you need to finish what you started?"

She looks at where my cock is still stood proud and wanting attention.

"Yes please." She says moving to take me back into her mouth.

"Oh fuck." I groan as she does it. Apparently spanking her turns me on too.

I let her work me up for a bit, enjoying the way her tongue swirls around me.

"Touch yourself Eden. Daddy wants you to cum too."

She does it quickly. She's such a horny little mess right now I barely get the words out before she's rocking her hips as she masturbates. But she keeps sucking me too. She doesn't show any dereliction of her duties and I lean back enjoying every second of this performance.

She's moaning more. Her throat is vibrating through me and just as my cum erupts into her mouth she cums, half gasping, half screaming and it pours down her lips.

"Oh Jesus." She says wiping her mouth and flushing with embarrassment.

"You're so fucking sexy." I say and she looks up at me grinning.

I swear if she hadn't have drained my balls so much I'd have a constant hard on from just the thought of her.

She gets in the shower and I join her, taking my time washing her body, massaging her tits. I'm not going to fuck her now but I want to enjoy every moment I have with her while I can.

Maybe I'm a lecherous old man. Maybe I am a pervert. But this girl does things to me I can't get my head around and for as long as she's willing to let me touch her I'm going to take every opportunity to do so.

When I meet up with Bob Aldross, I'm still thinking about her and I have to force the images from my head, force myself to focus on the seriousness of the conversation I'm about to have.

"I've looked through all the paperwork you sent over." Bob says.

"What do you think?" I ask.

He pulls a face. He's a hard man. A tough man. I've known him for years. He says what he thinks, he doesn't mince his words but he's so straight down the line and I like that too.

"Someone has definitely been taking a slice of pie for themselves."

"Shit." I mutter. Not that I didn't believe it but to hear if from an expert. It makes it more real.

"I'd like to get some of my boys to look into it. Do some digging. Nothing too obvious. We don't want to scare anymore or make any big waves."

"Do whatever you think is appropriate." I say. "I doubt we'll get the money back but I need to know who this is and I need you to do the proper investigations."

He nods. "I'll get right on it." He says. "I take it the Gala is still going ahead?"

"Yeah." I'd rather cancel it but I don't want to raise any eyebrows and besides it's all been paid for.

Christ the fucking Gala. I'd barely given it a moment's thought but Terri will be back by then. And we'll have to play the happily married couple while I spend the entire evening trying not to lust after Eden.

My phone buzzes and I pick it up to see the message from Eric. Clearly he's still pissed at me and evidently he's somehow found out I went away last weekend. From the message it's more than clear he's figured out what I was up too. That I was with Eden.

I swallow a groan. I should have kept my mouth shut because he's going to hound me now until I tell him I've done it. That I've dropped whatever this is.

Only I can't. I won't. I refuse to let her go now. We're both damned in this, both lost to our sin and I'm ready to ride this train to hell if that's what it takes just to enjoy whatever fleeting moments I get with my stepdaughter.

EDEN

Thirty-Three

"...So we were thinking of the eighteenth?" Katie says but I not really paying attention. I'm day dreaming, half staring out the window, imagining Dominic is walking down the road and I can ogle at him.

Except he doesn't really come to this part of the city.

He doesn't hang out in a student café. And he certainly wouldn't act like my boyfriend is we did bump into each other.

Not that I'd expect him to. But still, I prefer not to see him in public because it's easier for both of us. Less risky too.

God, how am I going to go back to playing the stepdaughter when mum comes back? I won't be able to walk around the house in just a thong. I won't be able to feel Dominic's arms as he grabs me at any given moment.

I won't be able to scream in full ecstasy as he makes me cum again and again and…

"Earth to fucking Eden."

"Huh, what?" I say blinking.

"Where the hell have you been just now?" She asks.

I grin. "Nowhere."

"Oh Jesus." She mutters.

"What?" I ask.

"You're fucking someone. And it's good isn't it?"

"What?"

"I can see it." She says. "The way you're holding yourself, the way you're practically glowing. Who is it?"

"You wouldn't believe me if I told you." I say back.

"So you are fucking someone." She says so loudly a few people look.

"Maybe." I say crossing my arms, sitting back in my chair and wincing at the slight pain from where Dominic spanked me this morning. He fucking spanked me. Damn do I want him to that again.

"Good." She says. "You deserve a bit of fun after that arsehole Aron."

"I thought you liked him?" I say. Hell she was the one pushing me in his direction in the first place.

"Yeah that was before…"

"Before what? Him treating me like shit? Him pushing me for sex all the time?"

"You do know why that was don't you?" She says.

"Why what was?" I ask.

"Him going on about having sex with you so much."

"Why?"

"Oh Eden." She says. "There was a bet."

"Excuse me?"

"Some of the guys were in on it but it was Aron's idea. They all reckoned you were still a virgin because no one has actually fucked you."

"The fuck?" I hiss.

"Yeah, so Aron made a bet that he could take your v-plates."

"You're not serious?" I snarl. "How long have you known about this?"

"Max told me the other day. He said he was pleased you'd dumped his arse and shown everyone what a piece of shit he is."

"How many others know?"

"Half of campus probably. Apparently Aron was very vocal about it at the end. Thought everyone would think he was some sort of stud."

"I'm going to kill him." I snarl.

"Why?" She says. "God Eden, tell me it's not him you're fucking."

"It's not. I wouldn't go near him with a barge pole."

"Then what does it matter? You're happy and he's walking around looking like the arsehole that he is because everyone knows you two didn't fuck and now half the girls won't even talk to him."

"Great. A real bit of feminine solidarity." I snap.

"I'm sorry Eden."

"It's okay. I just…" I shake my head. "I'm gonna head home, I've got to get going on my dissertation and I think I need a bit of space."

"Oh okay. Well let me know about this camping trip, that is if you're still up for it?"

"Maybe. Is Aron still going?" I ask.

"He's been uninvited."

I snort. "Let me think on it."

"We could do a girls weekend instead. Go to a spa?"

"Yeah that'd be good." I say. "I don't have much free time at the moment though. Mum's away and Dominic's got me on a curfew." It's a neat lie to ensure I maximise the time I've got with him.

"Urgh. Doesn't he know you're an adult? You can do what you want."

I smirk. Oh he is more than aware of that. And the thing I want to do most is him.

"Dads huh?" I joke and she agrees. Only she's not fucking hers.

DOMINIC

Thirty-Four

I walk in the house and though I know she's here it's quiet. Too quiet.

"Eden?" I call out.

"I'm in here." She says and I follow the sound until I find her sat in the orangery in the skimpiest dress I've ever seen.

"Jesus, do you dress like that to torture me?"

She lets out a giggle. "It's hot in here." Yeah it is. But only because she's sat with her legs open enough for me to see the wet patch already seeping through her underwear.

"What are you working on?"

"Nothing. Just my end of term dissertation." She says. Shutting it down and tossing the laptop onto the other couch.

I smirk as she gets up. "How was your day?" She asks.

"Long. Tough."

"Aww." She says putting her hands on my shoulders. "Would you like a little stress relief?"

"Are you offering?"

"I'm always offering Dominic. Why don't you sit down, make yourself comfortable and let me give you a proper welcome home?"

Fuck. The way the words roll from her mouth makes me want to face fuck her so badly. I look down at her dress. I'm not sure she's even wearing a bra right now. That or it's got no padding because I can see her nipples poking through.

I scratch them lightly, bringing them to full attention and she gasps for a second.

"Sit." She says.

"Are you taking charge tonight?" I tease.

"No. I'm just making sure you're properly taken care of."

I nod sinking into the couch as she starts to slip the dress from her shoulders. Maybe she's going to do a little dance, a strip tease just for me.

She rolls the fabric past her tits and they bounce with their new found freedom. Turns out she was braless. She then slides the fabric down before turning and bending over as she pulls it down over her perfect, pert little arse with a wiggle.

When the dress is off she turns around wearing nothing but a sheer diamante thong. I can see the top of her cunt through it and it's already sticking to her, giving me a perfect outline of how her lips hang.

"Come here. Come to Daddy." I say.

She steps up, straddling me, one thigh either side, with her tits right at eye level.

"Behaving like that, anyone would think you're after something." I murmur.

"Maybe I am." She half whispers.

I grin pulling a note from my pocket and tuck it into her thong. "There you go sweetheart."

"Seeing as I quit my job that'll come in handy." She replies.

"You quit your job?"

"I didn't have time for it, what with school work and homework…" She smiles with a glint in her eye. "And my extra-curricular activities."

"I thought you wanted to work?" I say. She's always been so fierce in defending it.

"I did but I want to spend time with you more and besides, I can always get another if I need it."

I nod. "Anything you need I can give you."

"Well Mr Mathers." She says taking my face between her hands. "What I need right now is for you to make me cum harder than I've ever cum before. Can you do that?"

I grin. Whatever the hell has gotten into her, I'm all for this.

She squeals as I pull her down on top of me against the base of the couch. "Ride my face." I say. "I'm going to eat you out until you squirt everywhere again."

"What if it ruins the couch?"

"Who cares? It'll be worth it." I say as I pull her thong to one side and half force her down onto my hungry mouth.

"Of fuck Dominic."

I suck hard to begin with. I'm going to edge her just a little, make her really want this before I grant her my mercy.

She's moaning, rocking her hips, literally riding me just like I told her.

And then I slow her down. I lick lighter, I tease. She throws her arms back behind her onto my chest and if anything it improves the angle for me.

My tongue flicks her clit. Her body clenches as I do it and I bring her so close to an orgasm I almost feel mean. Only I know the final crescendo will more than make up for it.

"Dominic." She gasps. Her nails are digging into me. She's desperate for me to end this.

I hold her right thigh, hold her body. With my spare hand I slide a finger into her arse. She jolts but she doesn't complain. I thrust inside, exploring this new part of her and she groans as I find her G spot.

She's squirming more now and I have to hold her tighter against my mouth because right now she's mine, my feast, my stress relief, my reward, and I'll take her how I want her, for as long as I choose too.

"Fuck please." She gasps.

I want to say something. To tease her. To taunt her but my mouth is far too occupied and I won't let the momentum drop for a quick jibe.

"Daddy." She gasps louder. "Let me cum. Please let me cum."

It takes all my effort not to laugh then. I suck once more, I roll her clit, I tease her, watching her face as best I can, watching her body as it falls to pieces.

GOOD GIRL

And then she jerks. Her moans turn to screams and she pulls as face of almost panic for a split second before her body flushes and she squirts all over my face. Just like the last time. And as I lay here drenched by it I know we have ruined the couch.

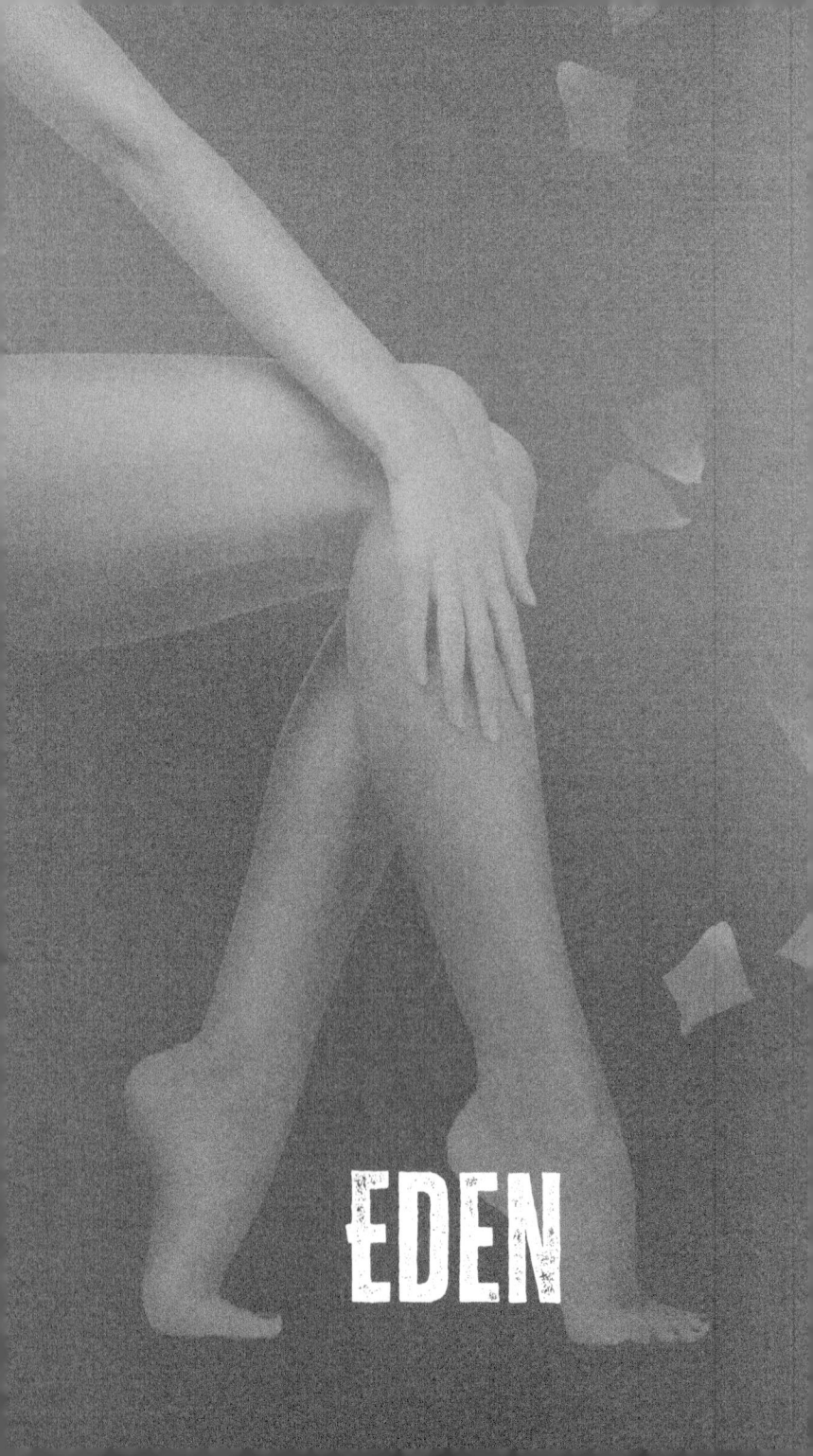

EDEN

Thirty-Five

I don't think I've stopped smiling all day. People must be noticing. Everyone must see it. I got the best grade on my assignment to date. Even my professors are commenting how great my new coursework is.

But more than that, bigger than that, Dominic is taking me out tonight. To dinner. It's our final hurrah and, though I know tomorrow everything will revert back to how it was, it feels like something fundamental has changed and besides, he's made it more than abundantly clear that he's got something special planned tonight.

It's a risk being out like this. We both know that but if we're careful any casual observers who know us will just see a kind stepfather taking care of his ward.

And what care he takes of me.

He bought me new underwear. Not that I've even gotten through the new ones I bought for our weekend away. And he says he has some other gifts too.

Somehow I know already that they're naughty. Toys probably. Maybe he bought a paddle to spank me with.

Fuck I hope he has.

When I get home from my last lecture he's already there, on the phone. Talking to someone.

"No. I agree." He says. His back is to me and I make a point of going into the kitchen because I don't want to eavesdrop.

"Yeah pull it. Pull it all Bob." He says following me.

The man on the other line says something. "I don't really care to be honest. Take whatever you need. At this point we just need answers."

The man replies and Dominic grunts before hanging up.

"Everything okay?" I ask. He's frowning, massaging his temples. He looks stressed.

"Yeah. Just some stuff with work."

"Same as before?" I ask.

He narrows his eyes. "I don't want to lie to you Eden."

"Then don't." I say. Shit where the hell is this going? Is he going to tell me this is over? Is he going to tell me that it's just a fling? That he's leading me on?

"There's some issues with work. Some has stolen money. A lot of money." He states.

"Do you know who it is?"

"No. The police are involved. But it's very hush hush right now."

"I won't say anything." I say. Christ, no wonder he's stressed.

"I know you won't but if I'm coming across as a dick, if I'm tense…"

"Then now I know why." I say stepping up to him and kissing him lightly. Only he kisses me back, grabbing me like he needs to hold me more than anything else.

"Is there anything I can do to help?" I ask.

"You're already doing more than enough." He says.

I smirk. I'm not. I'm not really doing anything.

"How about you get ready and then you can have one of your presents?" He says.

"Already?"

He grins and I swear I see a glint in his eyes.

I get ready quickly, putting the underwear he bought me on. It's got cut outs, my body is exposed to the point it's barely worth wearing it though mercifully it's not crotchless because the way this evening looks to be headed I'll need something to contain my arousal.

I put a bodycon dress on. It's tight, sexy but respectable enough if someone saw us.

Safety first and all that.

When I head back downstairs Dominic can't take his eyes off me.

"You look incredible." He says.

I blush. He's gotten changed too. He's wearing a dark silk shirt and trousers. He's undone the top buttons and I can see the hint of his chest. Damn is he oozing all silver fox vibes right now.

"Shall we go?" I murmur.

"Aren't you forgetting something?" He says.

"My present." I did forget.

He grins. "Bend over Eden."

"Excuse me?"

"Bend over." He says.

The fuck is this? I do it because why would I not. He pulls my dress up, tugs my thong aside and slips something into my ass.

"Oh shit." I gasp. It's cold. Hard, Not too big but enough that I can feel it.

"It's time we added to your lessons." He says putting my thong back, making me presentable again.

"By shoving things up my ass?"

He lets out a chuckle. "Tonight Eden I'm going to sit and eat and every time I get the urge I'm going to…"

I moan. I can't even help it. Something inside, that thing inside vibrates for a split second. He's shoved a god damn vibrator up my ass.

"Dominic." I begin.

He narrows his eyes. "Don't argue with me Eden."

"I'm not I just…"

"Do you trust me?"

I nod. Of course I trust him. But what if he takes it too far? We'll be in public.

"Then let's go. The taxi is waiting."

I bite my lip. I'm nervous. But he pulls me into his arms and kisses me. "Trust me. This is about your enjoyment."

"Promise you won't make me embarrass myself." I say.

He frowns. "I'll never do that."

DOMINIC

Thirty-Six

She's nervous. I can feel it. I can feel her keep eyeballing me.

Part of me likes it. Hell part of me loves it. I want her to be on edge, thinking about it, wondering when I'm going to strike, when I'm going to send another shock of pleasure through her.

But part of me, a bigger part wants to reassure her. Because it is about her pleasure, her enjoyment. I want her to have the spike of adrenaline, the rush of doing something so naughty, of being aroused in front of other people and yet, more than anything, I want her to have a good time.

I picked a restaurant I know well. The food is good. The place is ideally decorated with low lighting and best of all I got the table I want, in the corner.

When we're led to it I see her relax more. She's starting to believe that I'm not out to embarrass her.

I order a bottle of wine and I pour her a glass. After we've given our food choices I watch her. She's staring at me the way a rabbit does a viper that's about to pounce.

"When did you give up your job?" I ask.

She takes a sip of wine. "A few weeks ago. Before we went away."

"Why didn't you say anything?"

She shrugs. "I don't know. I guess a part of me didn't want to admit it. But you were right, I needed the time back, and anyway I got top marks for my last essay."

"The Milton one?"

She nods. "You remembered it."

"Of course I did." I say.

She smirks taking another sip of her wine. Is it wrong that I want her to get a little tipsy, maybe she'll relax more if she does. I take a sip of wine too. This isn't quite how I envisioned this night going. I'd thought she'd be more up for this than she is.

"Here." I say passing the remote over.

"What is it?"

"The control." I state.

"For the thing in my ass?" She half whispers.

"Yeah. Keep it."

She frowns. "Why are you giving this to me? I thought you wanted to…" She pauses as the waiter lays out our starters. Steak tartare for me and smoked salmon for Eden.

"I do." I say once he's gone. "But you're on edge. Uncomfortable. I'd rather you enjoyed this evening than I push something you don't want."

"And if I do want it?"

"Excuse me?"

"If I'm just nervous but I still want to play this game?" She says.

Fuck. She grins as if she can read my mind and her hand flits to the remote. I see her push the button, see her body move just a little and her mouth makes a perfect 'o' before she turns it off.

"Use it Dominic." She half gasps sliding it back to me.

"You're sure?" I say.

She grins more. "My body is your plaything this evening. Do whatever you want."

I grin too picking up the remote. Damn this girl is so fucking incredible. I push the button and she lets out a small moan as it hits her.

And then it stops. The pleasure goes and she stares back at me with those big brown eyes and her pupils so dilated.

My naughty little stepdaughter. Ready to let me use her in front of everyone of this city's prying eyes.

We eat our starter. I ask her more about her course and the dissertation she's working on. She takes her time to explain it, the research, the arguments. I want to push the button again but in this moment I'm so enraptured by her conversation I forget all about it.

Our main arrives and she tucks in greedily. I wonder if she's forgotten all about it.

"We have the Gala coming up." I say and she nods.

"Yeah I know."

"I want you there, if you're comfortable that is."

"I always attend. I think it would be noticeable if I wasn't showing my face don't you?" She replies.

I shrug. "You're old enough now to have an excuse if you want to bail."

"Do you want me to?" She asks.

"No. I want to see you dressed up. But I'll admit it won't be easy playing happy families."

"Tell me about it." She mutters and then she grins. "What about your toy?"

I raise an eyebrow.

"We could do a repeat of this evening. Maybe that might make your night easier?"

I laugh. "While I like the sound of that I wouldn't want to risk anything. We'll both have to be on our best behaviour I'm afraid."

She pulls a face. "I guess you'll have to make it up to me then."

"Will I now?" I reply.

"Yes Dominic." She says glancing at the remote and I can see where her head is. "So what do you say you start now?"

"Now?" I murmur hitting the button and she writhes.

"Yes." She gasps. Her hand grabs the table. Her glass shakes but she's not moaning and I haven't let off yet.

The waiter comes and clears our plates. She does her best to not show the fact she's falling apart right now and he doesn't seem to notice as the sweat literally builds on her brow.

"How's that for making it up to you?" I ask once he's gone and I turn it off.

She groans. Panting. "I think I just soaked my panties."

I laugh. "I hope so Eden because I'll be checking soon enough."

"Why not now? Let's skip dessert. I don't want anything else anyway."

"You want to go home?" I ask.

She nods. "I want you to take me home and finish whatever the hell you have planned for me."

I grin. Yeah she does. My naughty Lolita has had a hit and now she wants what only Daddy can give her.

I ask for the cheque. Leave them a more than generous tip and we walk out quickly. My hand is on the small of her back, guiding her. I probably should be more careful right now but I don't care. I'm lucky my erection isn't pinging out for half the neighbourhood to see and the whole way back in the taxi I've got her hand held on my groin feeling it though the driver can't tell from how I've draped my jacket.

We get in the house and she's kicking her shoes off, turning and kissing me like a woman possessed.

"I think you enjoyed that bit of exhibitionism." I say.

"Maybe I did Dominic. But I'm pretty certain whatever you're about to do I'll enjoy more."

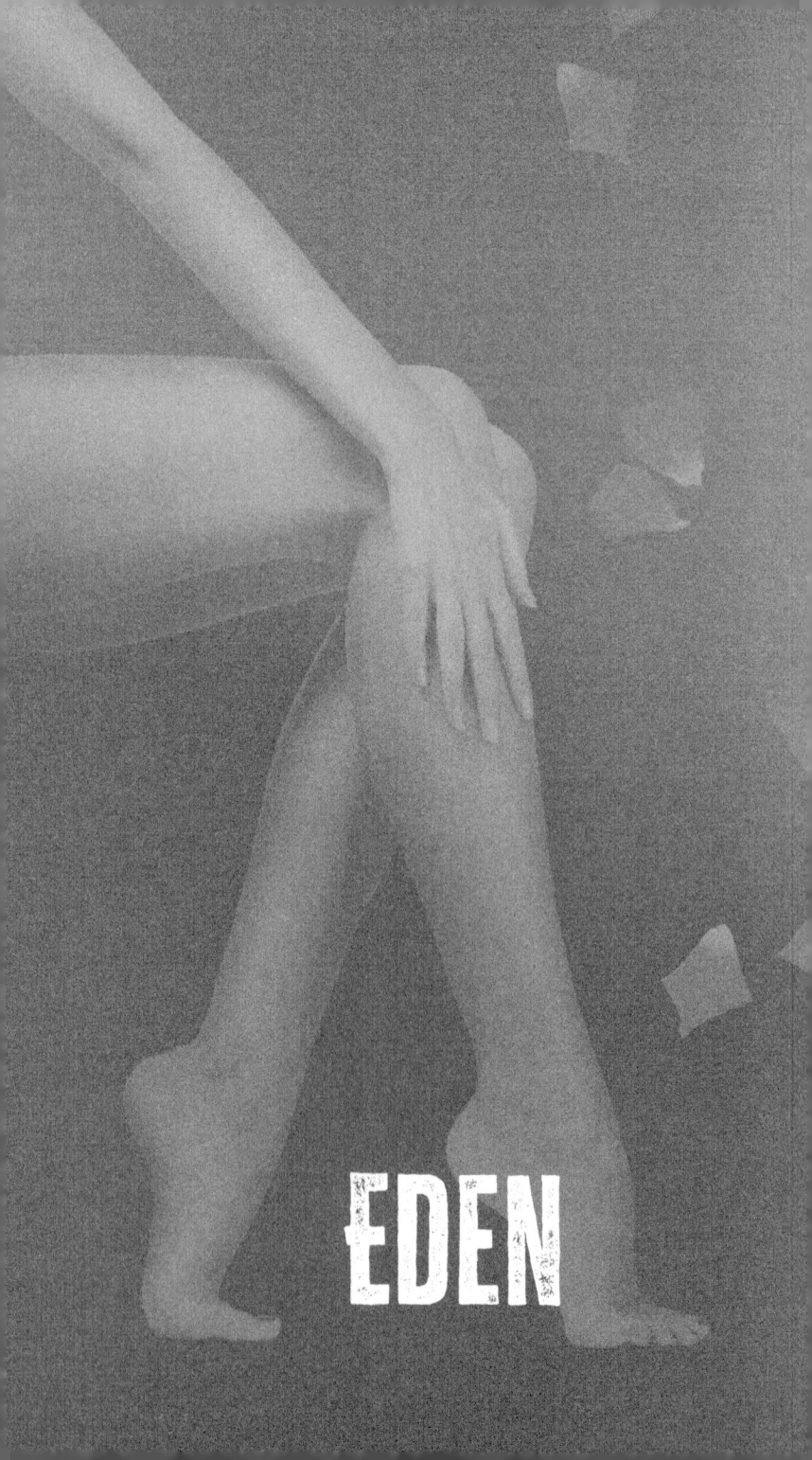

EDEN

Thirty-Seven

He unzips my dress and practically yanks it off me. I step back letting him admire the underwear.

He grins before hitting the remote in his pocket and I'm hit by a sudden wave of something incredible in my ass. I groan, grabbing hold of him only he tosses me over his shoulder and leaves me half writhing in his delicious torture as he carries me through his house.

He puts me down on the bed and as I pant he finally turns the damn thing off.

"That was mean." I say and he laughs.

"I'm just getting you prepped."

"For what?"

He runs his eyes over me. "I'm going to fuck you in the ass tonight Eden and you're going to love every minute of it."

I gulp. He's so certain right now and, while he's probably right I will like it, there's a tiny voice that says he hasn't even asked permission. He's just assuming I'd be okay with this.

"Don't you need to see if I want to first?" I say.

He pauses. "Do you not want to?"

I think my heart melts a little at the way he says it. At the way he suddenly becomes that concerned, protective man that I am falling so dangerously hard for.

"You want to." I say. "And I'm willing to try it."

"There's my good girl." He says. "But if you change your mind. At any point.."

"I know." I say before looking around. "Why are we in here?" I ask. We're not in my room. Not in his room either. It's one of the spare rooms. I doubt anyone's been in here in months. There'd be no reason to.

"Because tonight we're going to make a mess and by the time I'm finished with you, you'll be too tired for anything but just sleep." He says.

I swear my eyes widen at his words but he just kisses me. "Trust me." He says. "You're going to enjoy every moment of this."

I nod. "Tell me how you want me."

He grins, walking away and comes back with something in his hands.

It's a toy. A vibrator. The way he's been about my own one makes me surprised that he's even suggesting we use one now.

"To start with, you're going to fuck yourself while I cum all over you."

"What?"

"Lie down Eden. Show Daddy what you can do."

I hate to admit it but even the idea of this is hot. I get to pleasure myself while Dominic covers me in his cum? Yes please.

I grin lying back on the bed. Spreading my legs wide and turn the purple monster in my hand on. It hums as it comes to life and I start teasing my clit. Rubbing it against myself.

"Like this Daddy?" I say.

"That's a start." He says climbing on the bed and kneeling between my legs watching. "But you actually have to stick it in Eden." He says.

I look up at him. I've never done that, never put a toy inside me. And then I remember the vibrator he shoved in my ass hours ago. The toy that's still there even now, although it's dormant.

"Do it with me." I say.

He takes my hand, controlling the movement, plunging the toy inside. His eyes fixed on where it's sinking between my lips.

"Your cunt is so perfect." He murmurs.

"Watch me fuck it then." I say and I start moving the toy in and out.

It's so different to Dominic. It's harder, there are nodules all along it that hit some sort of pleasure spots in me. I let out a moan and shut my eyes for a moment.

"Does that feel good sweetheart?" He asks.

"Soo good." I gasp.

"Better than Daddy's cock?"

I shake my head. "Nothing is better than your cock Daddy."

He grins. "That's right Eden. You love my cock don't you?"

"Yes." I say picking up speed.

"Such a good girl. You always know how to make Daddy happy."

"I want to. I want to make you so happy."

"Oh you do Eden. No one makes me happier than you." He says grabbing my face, kissing me hard.

"Dominic." I gasp but he's already pulling away from me, sitting back on his haunches to watch the show between my legs.

He's groaning now. I realise he's wanking himself off and I open my eyes to watch. He's just so fucking hot. His biceps are bulging, his stomach is taunt. I can see the way his skin is glistening over his six pack and those tattoos of his.

"Where do you want me to cum on you Eden?"

"On my face." I say.

He raises his eyebrows "Really?"

"Yes. Cum all over my face, then cum again over the rest of me."

He shakes his head slightly. "My Lolita is very demanding this evening." He says amused but I can hear he's close now.

"Please Daddy please. Cum all over me and then fuck me in the ass."

He groans, moving quickly, grabbing my body as he leans over and I stare at his perfect, veiny dick as he starts spurting all over my face.

"Oh god." I moan. It's incredible. I can feel it sticking to my skin, to my eyes, I can smell it too as it soaks into my pores.

I can hear him panting. He's still close to my head.

"You look incredible right now." He murmurs.

I flush. "Thank you Daddy." I say blinking to get his cum out of my lashes. "Thank you for my reward."

He chuckles. I'm still technically fucking myself but my pace has dropped.

He moves back between my thighs and takes over for a bit, alternating between rubbing over my clit and thrusting into me. It's incredible. Lying here, letting him do what he wants.

I know soon he'll have had enough rest and he'll be able to cover the rest of me.

As I start to feel my orgasm grow he takes his dick back in his hand. He's rubbing himself but I can see he's still too soft.

"I'm going to cum." I gasp.

"Good girl. Cum as many times as you can." He says kissing my thigh. "I want this to be a night neither of us forgets." Like I've forgotten any of the nights I've been with him. Like I could even try.

I nod. I'm biting my lip. He's still in control, still working away with the toy and I stare at him, moaning more and more as I start to give in.

"That's my girl." He says as I start to scream. His hand is moving more. He's getting hard again.

"Cover me." I gasp.

"I will Eden." He says. "All in good time."

DOMINIC

Thirty-Eight

I hear her groan. She's desperate for me. Desperate for me to cover her more.

Christ, could she be more perfect?

I look up at her face, seeing the way my cum covers it. She's magnificent. She's resplendent. She keeps licking her lips as if she needs the taste of it on her tongue. As if it's a sugar hit. As she's some sort of addict.

I'm getting harder. I'm recovering quicker. I guess my body is adapting to this new found demand and all those months of simply jacking off in the shower is now little more than a memory. A nice hiatus for my balls. But not anymore.

She's taken over the toy again. I groan watching as her greedy little cunt welcomes it in over and over. As her lips suction around it, as her body writhes with each new penetration.

She's a work of art. She's the most exquisite dancer. I watch her tits, watch as they bounce.

Fuck I want to bite her nipples so hard. I lean over and suck one in.

She gasps moaning at this new sensation. I'm giving her a hiccy I realise. I sucking so much she'll bear the mark for days.

"Cum on me." She begs again.

She's such a needy little thing right now. Such a sweaty mess for me.

"Lay flat, you don't want to waste any." I say and she does. Obeying me instantly.

I move back leaning over her. I'm not quite ready yet but she doesn't know that and I stare watching at her face. She's so expectant. She's so excited. It's like I've promised her a miracle and she's now waiting for me to perform it.

"Such a good girl." I mutter.

"Your girl." She says.

"My girl." I agree.

She's slowing down.

"Are you ready for your next reward Eden?"

"So ready." She says. "Please Daddy. Please let me have it."

I groan, my dick is throbbing with its need, my balls are constricting more and more and as I lean over her I cover her tits, cover her entire chest as she moans and moans like a thing possessed.

I lay panting over her. She's tossed the toy now. She's laying there staring back at me.

"Do you like the feel of my cum Eden?"

"I love it." She gasps.

I stay where I am, watching her. And then I get up and grab the remote for the toy she's forgotten about. The one still up her ass.

I flick it on and she gasps, her legs jerking.

"Oh shit."

"Relax." I murmur. "We need to get you nice and ready for my cock."

She nods. Her body is writhing. She's rocking her hips as if she's humping something.

"Do you like the feel of it?" I ask.

"Yeah." She breathes and I laugh.

"Just wait till my cocks in you. You're going to like it even more." I promise.

She nods again. "I'm ready." She says. As if she knows what's about to hit her. As if she has a fucking clue.

My cock's getting harder but it's not good to go.

And then an idea hits me. I move round, grabbing her cum covered face.

"Make Daddy hard for you." I murmur as I slip it into her mouth. "Get him nice and ready for your arsehole."

She grins up at me, her tongue springing to action as it caresses my cock.

Fuck she's an angel. Within minutes she's worked her magic enough for what I need. What she needs too.

I pull out and she stares back at me. "Now?"

I nod.

She goes to roll over, as if I'm going to fuck her like a dog.

"No Eden." I say grabbing her quickly to stop her.

"You look so beautiful right now we don't want to ruin it do we?"

She frowns confused and I pull her up to her feet moving to sit in front of the big mirrored wardrobe with her stood in front of me.

"Look at yourself. Look how good you look with my cum all over you."

She grins, running a finger through a drip that's coming off her nipple and she raises it and sucks it clean.

I smirk. She's such a whore for my cum but I wouldn't have it any other way. I pull her ass cheeks and take the vibrator out, tossing it.

And then I grab the lube. She's going to be tight. Even after all our prep work she's going to be tight. I pour it all over my cock, rub it all over.

"You're going sit on me." I say. "You're going to sit your ass on my cock and watch as I fuck you."

Her eyes widen but she's obviously all for it.

I grab her hips, positioning her at a slight angle. Her tits hang so delectably as I do it. And slowly I push my cock in through her arsehole. She gasps, I can feel her tensing then trying to relax.

She's tight but god does she feel good.

"How's that?" I ask.

She nods.

"Sit down then." I say. "Take me properly like a good girl."

She sinks onto me, her ass cheeks colliding with my skin as she groans.

I pull her head up, hold it so that she's staring at herself and then I start to thrust.

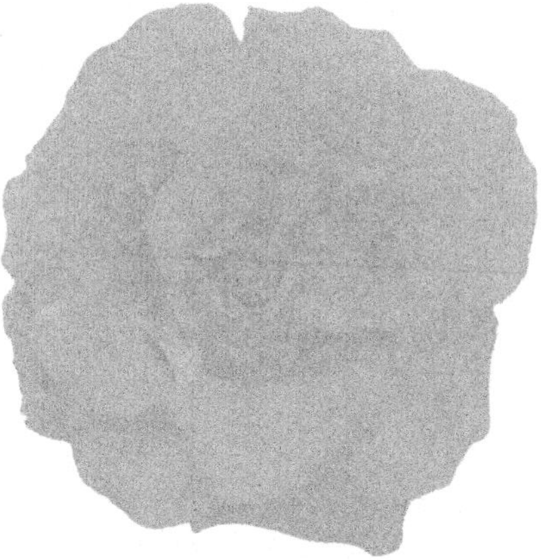

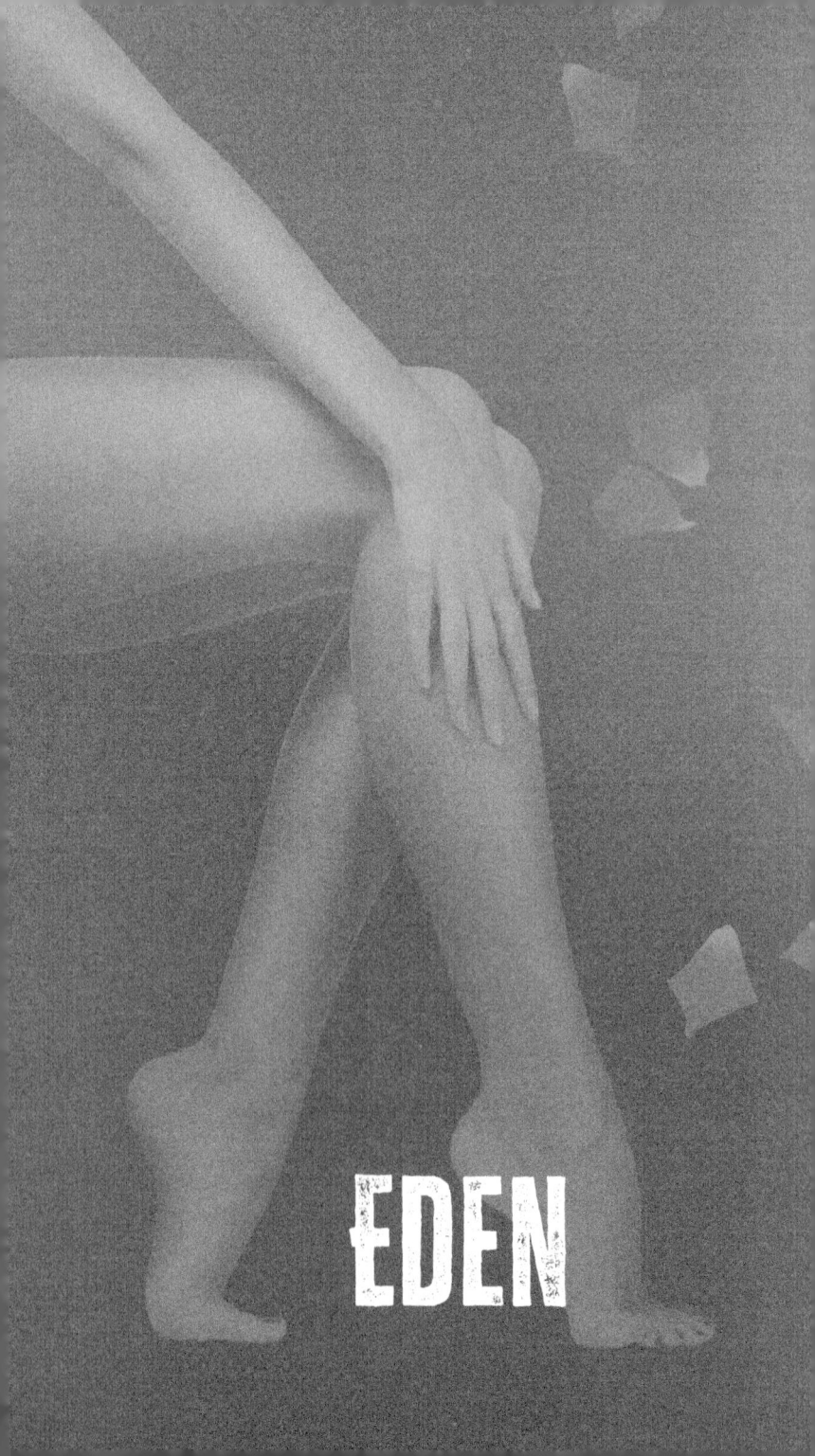

EDEN

Thirty-Nine

He's in my ass. He's in my ass right now.

I'm staring at myself. Staring at him too as he's fucking me. I was expecting pain. I was expecting it to feel similar to the first time we had sex but it's so different.

It's uncomfortable but not unpleasant. And, as he's sliding into me more and more, I can feel it turning to something akin to pleasure.

Oh Christ I am enjoying this.

I look back, I meet his eyes in the mirror. He's staring at me, watching my face, no doubt wanting to see if I'm okay with this or if he needs to stop.

"Harder Daddy." I say. "Fuck me harder."

He grins kissing my shoulder and then by god he does it.

It feels incredible. It feels unimaginable. I lean my head back, arch my back, roll my hips as he bottoms out and I let out such a moan.

"Look how beautiful you are." He says and I do. I stare at myself, at how my breasts are heaving, at how far my nipples poke out, at how my face shows the complete and utter ecstasy that I'm in, but most of all I see his cum, all over me, dripping down my cheek, drenching my skin.

He pulls my legs so that they're up over his and my pussy is completely exposed. I watch as he starts teasing my clit, as he runs his fingers down me, as he continues fucks me.

"Dominic." I moan.

"Tell me how good it feels Eden."

"It's so good. It's so fucking good." I cry.

"How does it feel to have my cock in your ass?"

"Don't stop. Please don't stop."

"Beg me properly Eden." He says.

"Please Daddy." I gasp. I'm so close. I'm so exhausted too. I'm at the very edge of my limit at the very cusp of what I can handle.

He wraps his other hand around the front me, gripping my shoulder and he kisses me behind my ear.

And then I feel it. The same feeling as before. The feeling that I'm going to piss myself. I whimper slightly. I know what it is now but for a split second I still have the fear.

"Dominic…" I gasp and he nods grinning. He knows what's about to happen too. He can see it. He can probably feel it.

My body jerks and I moan so deeply as it flushes through me. I've squirted again. I've squirted everywhere, over his fingers, over our legs. It runs between where his cock is still embedded inside me.

"What a good girl." He says. "Squirting all over Daddy like that."

I nod. I'm still right on the edge. Right on the verge of cuming and his fingers haven't relented, haven't stopped.

I grip his thighs, I dig my nails into them and as my body completely and utterly disintegrates I hear him growl and I feel it too, him cuming into my ass.

We collapse in a heap. Me on top of him. And we lay for what feels like forever as our sweat mixes and pools between us.

He was right we did make a mess but right now I don't even have the energy to shower his cum off from where it's dried all over my skin and in all honesty I don't want to either.

DOMINIC

Forty

I hear the door click. I hear the sound of her calling out.

I feel like such an arsehole as my heart sinks but I turn around smiling anyway. Like the fraud that I am. Like the shit that I am.

"Hey." I say.

"Hey Dom." She says, dumping her suitcase. She looks exhausted. She looks almost green around the gills.

"Are you sick?" I ask her.

She shakes her head. "No. it's just been a long two weeks."

"Let me make you a drink then." I hear myself say as if on autopilot.

"Non-alcoholic. I've drunk so much of late." She says.

I raise my eyebrows. When has my wife ever turned down a drink? Still, her drinking less would be a vast improvement.

"Here you go." I say passing her juice.

She smiles taking it. "Where's Eden?"

"At the library. She's got a dissertation she's finishing up." In truth I think she's hiding out there but I don't blame her. If I could I'd do the same right now. It'd certainly be easier than playing the doting husband.

"How's she been?"

"Fine." I say.

"And she's studying properly again?"

"She never stopped. She's a good kid." I state and internally cringe because she's not a kid. She's a grown woman, studying for a degree. Christ, who am I trying to convince there?

She's my stepdaughter.

And I've been fucking her nonstop since Terri left. And my only regret right now is that when she gets home I won't be able to bend her over this island and fuck her relentlessly until she's lost her voice from screaming so much.

Terri nods. "How about we go out for dinner, just the two of us?"

"Would you like that?"

She smiles. "We never spend any time together of late. I think it would be good too."

I swallow the feeling in me. As much as I want to make an excuse I can hardly turn her down right now. And besides there's nothing wrong with just a meal. Nothing untoward in itself. And yet it feels…

"We could eat here." I hear myself saying. "I could cook. You look tired anyway."

"Okay then." She says pulling a bar stool. Christ she's never given in like that before.

I smile. "Why don't you go take a shower? I'll start cooking something now."

She gets up and goes and I frown wondering, hoping, god praying, that she's not making some weird attempt at rekindling this relationship because we both know it's been dying a slow death for well over a year.

She comes back just as I'm ready to serve up. She's wearing a silk robe. Her hair is down. She looks beautiful but as I look at her all I can think of is that I wish it was her daughter opposite me. I wish it was Eden.

"Here you go." I say putting the plate of fettuccini in front of her.

She barely waits for me to sit before she's tucking in. Maybe that's where Eden gets her love of food from. Fuck, I shake the thought out of my head because I don't want to compare them. It feels wrong.

Perverted almost.

The mother and the daughter. I've fucked them both.

"Tell me about your project." I say and she does. She explains in great depth about the client, about the marketing plan, the budget. I can see she's passionate and it makes me remember how she used to be, how we used to be, when we were first dating.

I make a joke about some place we went years ago. She laughs.

"What about that trip to Hawaii we went on?" She says. "The one that you pitched as five star."

"It was according to the website." I say and we both laugh.

And then I hear the door click. I can't help it, I look up and my eyes meet hers. She gives me a small secretive smile before heading over.

"Welcome home mum." She says as I try not to study her face, as I try not to act suspiciously.

"We're just having dinner. Do you want some? I've made enough." I say.

"No I'm good." Eden says. "I ate something already. And I have some studying to do."

"Then why don't you leave us to it?" Terri says. "Get on with whatever work you're supposedly doing."

"Terri." I say. She hasn't seen her daughter in two weeks and already she wants her gone? Christ, was a mother she is.

"It's okay. You two have fun." Eden says looking at me in particular as if she's trying to give some sort of signal that none of this shit bothers her but it bothers me. Terri has no right to talk to anyone like that, let alone her own daughter.

I watch as she disappears but just as she reaches the stairs she looks back and gives me a small smile. She's a better person than me. A lot better person than me.

"She'll get over it." Terri says. "She needs to learn."

"Learn what exactly?" I ask looking back at my wife.

"That not everything in this house revolves around her."

"Why do you treat her like that?" I ask.

"Like what?"

"Like she's beneath you?"

Terri frowns for a second. "She's a child Dominic."

"She's your daughter."

She just stares at me as if I'm insane, as if I'm the uncaring one.

I get up to clear the plates and her arms tuck around me as I put them in the sink. Jesus Fucking Christ.

"Shall we go to bed?" She murmurs.

"What's gotten into you?" I ask turning to face her.

"Nothing." She sighs putting her hands on my chest. "I just think we've spent so much time apart of late and it's made me realise how much I miss you."

"Terri…"

"I want to rebalance my life. Spend more time with you."

"Why now?"

She shrugs. "I guess it feels like time's running out."

"On what?"

She stares up at me, tilting her head. "Us having a baby."

"Excuse me?" I say. For years I wanted kids, hell I still do on some level, but Terri made it clear from the get go she wasn't interested and at the time I thought she'd change her mind. Only she kept stating what a mistake Eden was and she wouldn't make the same one twice. I guess I should be grateful for that now because if we had a child together it would make this whole situation even more of a car crash.

But now suddenly she wants to have a baby? She's about to turn forty. She really wants to have baby at this stage in her life? The fuck is going on?

"I want us to be a family." She says.

"We are a family." I say.

"I want us to start our own family. You and me."

"What about Eden?"

"What about her?" She hisses.

"She's part of this family too." I snap.

"Why are you always so concerned with Eden these days?" She says. "I'm the one you're married too. Maybe you should look out for your wife more."

I don't even know how to respond I just stare at her.

"Dominic you want children. You've always wanted children. Why don't we start trying? We could have a baby, be happy again."

"A baby doesn't fix the issues we have." I state.

"So you admit that there are issues." She says stepping back, folding her arms.

"Of course there fucking are." I snarl. Christ I'd be an idiot not to know it.

"Okay, well how about we work on the intimacy and maybe the rest will fix itself."

"Are you that desperate for sex right now?" I growl.

"Maybe I am Dominic. Maybe I miss my husband and want to feel what it's like to be wanted." She's touching me again. And in this moment I can't stand it.

"No, don't pull this shit." I say.

And she huffs storming off before I can get another word in.

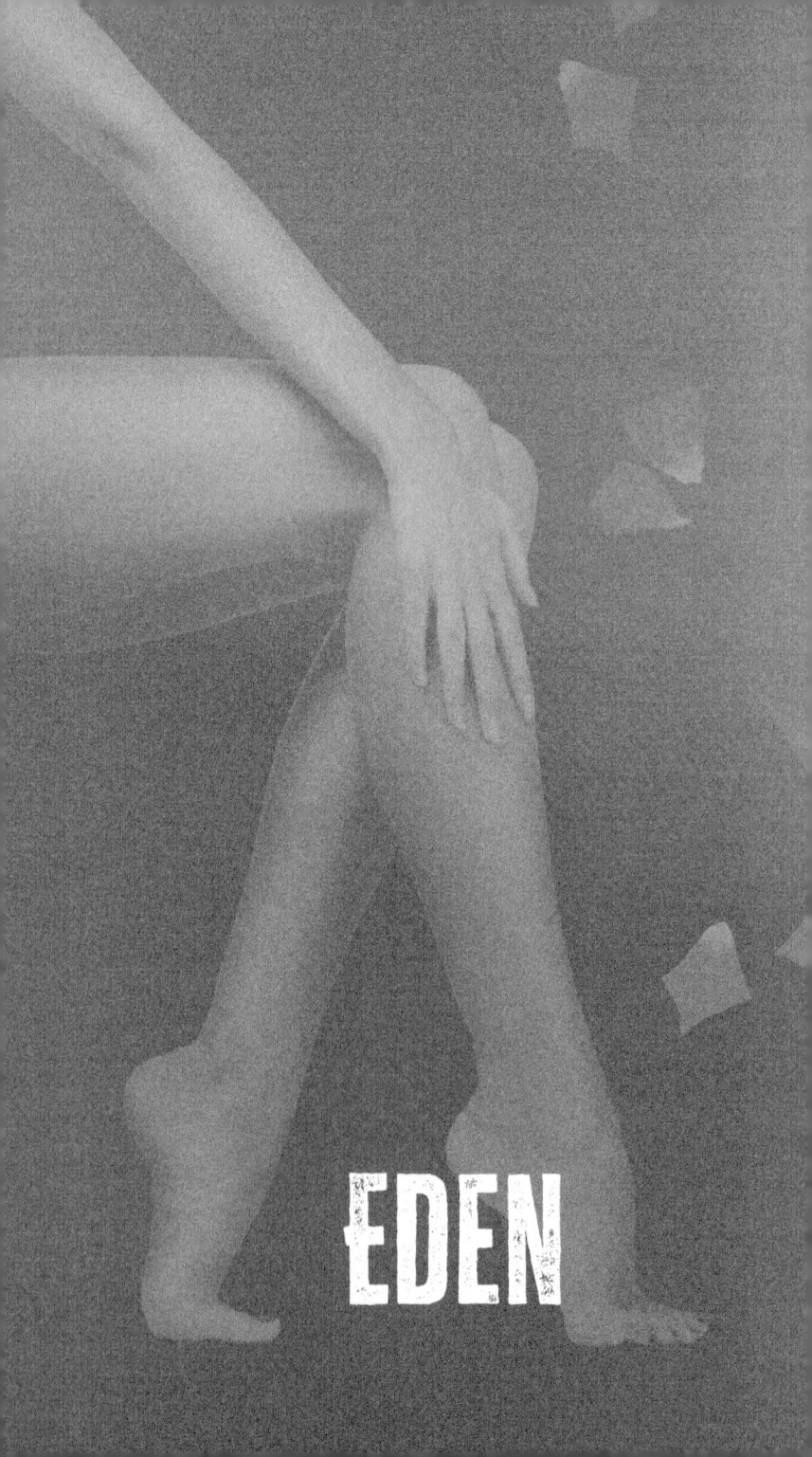

EDEN

Forty-One

She's been back a week. And by god has it been the slowest, worst week of my life.

I've spent the majority of it out of the house, out of the way, and though the benefit of it is I'm not seeing my mother, I'm also not seeing Dominic either and my nerves are starting to fray.

The way she was the night she got back, the way she was looking at Dominic, talking to him, it makes me feel so angry and so jealous and I hate that I'm becoming that person.

And if I'm honest there's a tiny part of me that's scared Dominic will change his mind, that he'll see my mother paying him attention and he'll remember all the good times, all the happy times, he'll remember what they were and he won't want to lose it.

If I admit it, I'm scared he'll forget about me.

So I've spent every waking hour buried in my degree work, focusing on a dissertation that's not even due in for another two months and yet I'm almost done. Almost finished.

I guess I should be grateful. It's the last bit of coursework and while all my classmates are starting to panic because they haven't even started, I'm already getting mine reviewed on its first draft.

But that's also the reason I'm home now. Because I can hardly work on something while my professor is going through it with a fine tooth comb.

I'm sat, in the snug, working on something I've not looked at in a long while. It's a story I wrote, a novel, except it needs a lot of reworking and I guess now I have the time to do it. If I can get it done, if I can get it into something that I'm happy with, I might even have the balls to send it off to some literary agents and perhaps, just perhaps, I might be able to achieve my dream of being a writer.

Although I doubt it'll be that easy. Most writers get a heap of rejections before they finally get somewhere. But that's okay. I'm used to rejection. I'm used to criticism and I know long term, if I keep pushing, eventually I'll make it. Because something in my gut tells me that.

"Hey." Dominic says and my heart jumps at his voice.

I look up at him, running my eyes over his body before I can stop myself.

"Hey." I say smiling.

"You've been away a lot."

I nod. "I've been working on my dissertation." I say. "And hiding too." I admit.

He sighs sitting down. "I thought so. I'm sorry."

"For what?" I ask.

"For this. For complicating this."

"You didn't do this. It was us. Together." I state.

He nods. "I was hoping to see you. I was going to message you. I got you something. An early birthday present."

"What?" I say pulling a face. My birthday isn't for another month. It's not just early, it's ridiculous.

"I thought it might be a way to cheer you up too."

"I'm not sad." I say.

"No?" He teases leaning in and as his lips get close it's all I can do not to kiss them. He must see the way I'm looking at him because he smirks for a moment. "I miss you." He says.

"I miss you too." I say and then suddenly he is kissing me, his hands are wrapped in my hair and I'm throwing my laptop aside falling on top of him, grinding my hips against him.

He groans, his hands running up my leggings and grasping my ass.

"Fuck." I hear him say.

"Will you?" I say lifting my head.

"Right now?" He says.

"Yes. Fuck me. Prove this wasn't all in my head." I say before I can keep the words down.

"Of course it isn't." He snaps but he's pulling my leggings down anyway, freeing his dick and thrusting into me so quickly, so forcefully, my eyes practically roll back.

"Oh god." I moan. I don't even know where my mum is, if she's in the house, if she's even home. Hell, if she walked in on us now I don't think I'd care, I certainly wouldn't stop. I'd be fucking Dominic anyway, showing her exactly what we are to each other.

It's like I've lost all control. Like I've gone mad. Maybe I am the whore I think I am. Maybe I am the slut Timothy called me but right now all I know is I need Dominic.

I need him in this moment.

I need him more than life itself.

DOMINIC

Forty-Two

This wasn't meant to happen. I wasn't meant to be fucking her right now. I just, I don't know. One minute she was looking at me and then I couldn't control it. I had to touch her, to feel her, to be in her.

I can feel her body against mine, even through all the clothes we still have on. I can feel the way her cunt is latching onto me. She's half rabid, she's clawing at me, biting, riding me like a woman possessed and as I fuck her back just as hard I wouldn't want it any other way.

This entire week I've ached for her. I've dreamt of her. I've walked through every room in the house hoping she'd be there, with that beautiful smile and those beautiful eyes. I stare at all the places we've had sex, I've got one of her jumpers hidden away where Terri can't find it and I smell it, smell her.

And I spend hours in the shower, wanking myself off to the memories of her body, to the memories of her laugh. To the very smell of her.

She's moaning more and more. I know Terri will be home soon and a part of me, a stupid part wants her to see this. For it all to end. For us to be found out and for it finally to be out in the open.

"Oh fuck, oh fuck, oh fuck." She gasps and I grip her tightly. She's about to cum. She's about to start screaming and as her walls contract around me I feel myself topple off the edge.

"Cum Eden." I growl as I pump into her and she does, like my perfect fucking angel, she cums, screaming and writhing and leaking out all over us.

When we're done she's quick to get off me. I guess we both come to our senses as our lust and our need subsides. She pulls her clothes back on, but she sits, half panting and staring at me still.

"I didn't mean to do that." I say.

"No?" She replies. "You didn't want to fuck me again is that it?"

I frown. "Of course I do. I just don't want you to think that's all I want."

She smirks. "I think I know you well enough now to know you're not just after sex." She states. "Besides you haven't considered the alternative? That maybe I was just using you."

I let out a laugh. She grins and it half takes my breath away.

"How about that present then?" I say.

"You're sure it's not too early?"

"It'll make sense when you see it." I reply before getting up to go get the impulsive present I know she'll love and Terri will absolutely hate.

She gasps when she sees it, in my arms, squirming to get free.

"A dog?"

"You've always wanted one." I say and she nods.

"Wait, what will mum say?" She says. Terri's always been so against pets. A waste of money she calls them.

"Do you care?" I ask.

She lets out a laugh. "Not really."

"Then neither do I." I say passing the tiny German Shepherd to her. The puppy stares up at her and then half rolls over as she starts tickling it.

"What do you want to call him?" I ask.

She grins. "I don't know."

"What about Milton?" I say.

"Milton?" She says frowning.

"From that book you were reading."

She lets out a laugh. "Milton." She tries it out loud, looking at the puppy to see if it suits. "I like that."

"So it's a good early present?" I say.

"It's perfect." She replies.

"What is that?" Terri says behind us and we both jump. "Is that, is that a dog? Dominic?" She says narrowing her eyes at me.

"It's a present for Eden. For her birthday." I state.

"Her birthday isn't until August." She says. "And I would have thought you would've discussed such a purchase with me first. You know how I feel about animals."

Eden half scowls at her, wrapping her arms around the puppy protectively.

"I don't really give a fuck what you think." I say before I can stop myself and Terri's jaw drops but I keep going. Hell I've dug a hole now, I might as well bury myself. "This is Eden's home and if she wants a puppy, hell if she wants a dozen puppies then she can have them." I state.

Terri just stands gaping at me and then turns on her heel storming off.

But Eden's shaking her head. "You shouldn't have said that."

"Why?" I ask. Is she annoyed that I defended her? Surely not.

"Well for one thing you've pissed her off." Eden says getting up, but keeping hold of Milton, cradling him like a baby.

"And two?" I ask.

"I might just demand eleven more puppies." She says before kissing me lightly and walking away.

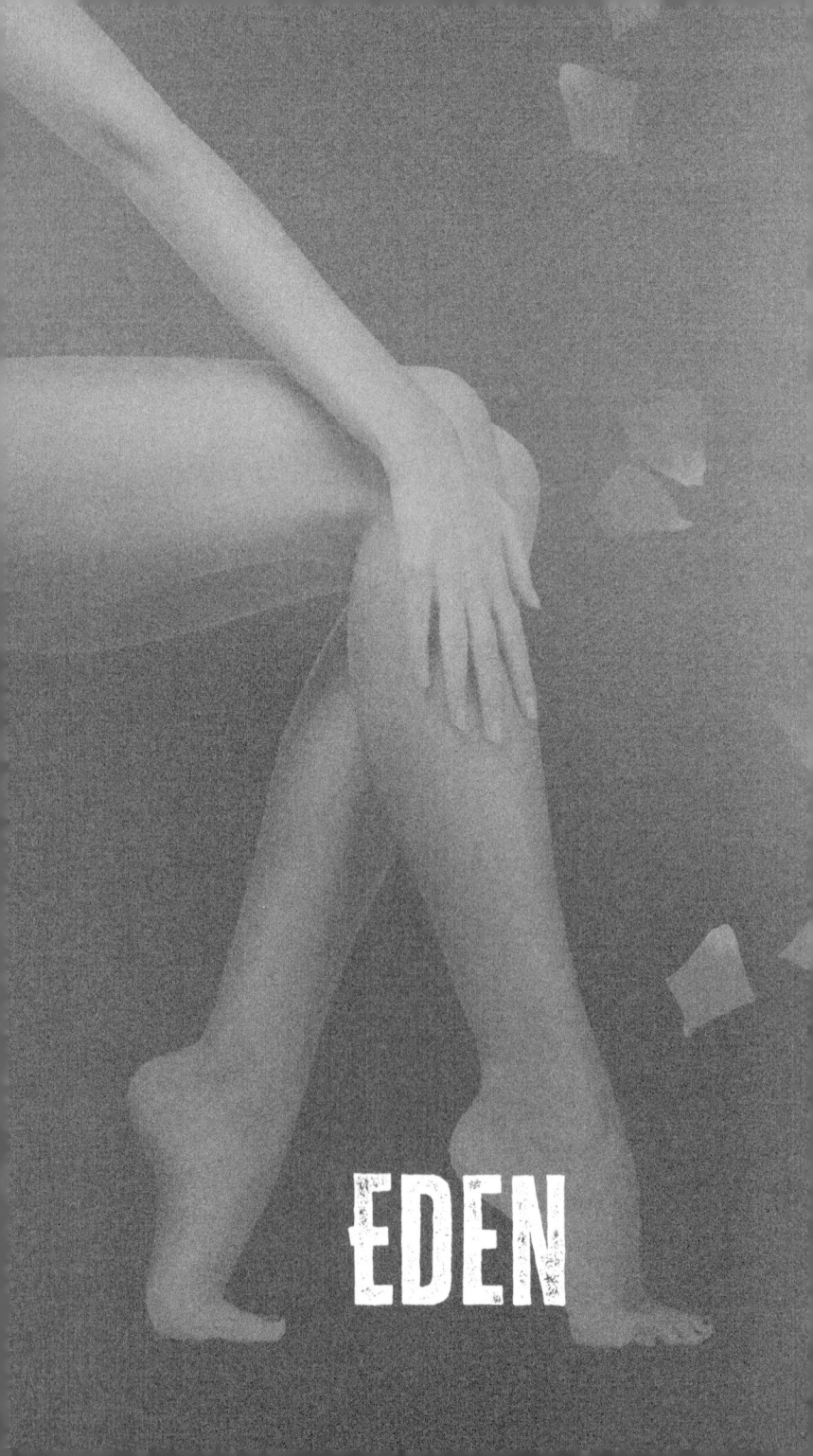

EDEN

Forty-Three

My dissertation is back and while I have a lot of feedback to go through, I'm sat with Katie in the library helping with hers. She's not even doing the same degree as me, she does history, but I'm going through books, pulling out anything I think can help.

We've drunk more than is a reasonable amount of coffee. And I've also spent an inordinate amount on chocolate and sweets. We should both be on a sugar high right now but I guess class struggles of early twentieth century Russia are enough to take that out of anyone.

Katie sighs slamming her book shut.

"I'm so bored of this. Why did I even choose this subject?" She moans.

"Because you love history and you love the Russian Revolution." I say.

"Yeah remind me of that once I've written twenty thousand words on the damn topic."

I laugh. "You did get to pick your own question Katie."

"Fuck off." She says. "Miss goody two shoes over here with your dissertation already done."

"Hey, I've got to make all the amendments and add more sources." I reply.

"Yeah sounds real tough." She says.

I laugh. "Another coffee?"

"Nah I really need to head off if that's okay with you? Max and I are going out to a new restaurant tonight. " She says.

"Sure. I think I'm all Russia'd out now anyway." I say slamming the books shut and stuffing my things into my bag.

We walk back to where I've parked my car as she continues to moan about her dissertation and how far behind she is on it. When she gets in she pulls her phone out and then groans.

"What's up?" I ask seeing the disgruntled look on her face.

"Max. He's running late from practice. So much for a romantic date." She grumbles.

"How're things with you two?" I ask. I know things have been strained. He's been picked by a local county team and is going on tour with them, meaning he'll be on the road for god knows how long.

"Yeah they're okay." She says. "We're actually talking about moving in together."

"Seriously?" I say.

"Yeah." She grins. "We're just waiting to see how we cope with the tour but if we can make it work over the summer then we're going to look at apartments."

"Oh my god Katie. That's amazing."

"My parents aren't too happy. They think I'm moving too fast but we've been together for four years. It's not exactly a new relationship."

I nod. "They'll come round."

"What about this mystery guy then?" Katie asks. "Are you still seeing him?"

"Yeah." I say. "It's complicated though."

"How come?"

For a second I consider telling her but my gut says keep quiet. Because what exactly do I expect her to say back if I admit I'm fucking my stepdad? She'll hardly high five me and say good on you.

"I, I don't want to lie to you but I can't tell you why either." I murmur as we pull out from the car park and onto the main road.

She pulls a face. "Eden, who is he?"

I shake my head. Keeping my eyes focused on the road in this moment because it's easier than looking into my best friends face.

"Is he some sort of criminal, is that it?" She asks.

I burst out laughing. "I think you've seen too many episodes of Criminal Minds."

"Can I at least meet him?"

"Not a chance." I say.

"Why not Eden?" She says folding her arms.

"Look, I know you've got my back but right now it's really early days and apart from anything else I don't want to jinx it." I say.

"You really like him though?"

"I do. Probably too much." I say the last bit and wonder how true that statement is. I guess time will tell.

"Eden, the way you're being all weird right now…"

"I know." I say turning to look at her for a moment. "I don't mean to be. And I promise you I will be honest as soon as I can but it's complicated."

Out of the corner of my eye I see the flash of colour. I look to my right then. I turn my head to the side and see the vehicle hurtling towards us despite the lights being green for me. I half gasp as I realise it's going to collide.

That it's going to crash right into the side of my car and there's nothing I can do to stop it.

I want to say something, to tell Katie to duck. I want to cry out, but I can't do anything but stare as the mass of metal gets closer and closer and closer.

DOMINIC

Forty-Four

"You went to the cops?" Timothy says walking in and half slamming the door shut behind him.

I sigh sitting back in my chair. I don't know how he found out but I guess it doesn't matter now. "I didn't have a choice."

He narrows his eyes. "I told you I was handling it."

"No, you said you were looking into it. But I'm sorry Tim, that's not good enough. If someone is embezzling trust funds we have to report it. We have a legal duty to."

He smirks.

"Do you really?" He says.

"What the fuck are you saying?" I growl. "Of course we do. Because apart from anything else we have to find out who it is."

"And if we know who it is?"

"Do you?" I ask.

He pulls a face, and then slides something across the desk at me.

I frown opening it up. Seeing countless photographs. It feels like a ton of bricks hits me. It feels like I'm suddenly stunned into silence and yet wanting to go berserk all at the same time.

I flick through, even as my hands shake. It's Eden. It's me. It's both of us. He's got pictures. Dozens of them. There's Eden, straddling me as I'm tucking that god damn twenty pound note into her thong. There's one of her obviously sucking me off. One with her bent over the table and dozens more.

Jesus Christ he must have stalked us for days.

"The fuck is this?" I growl.

I thought you said you weren't messing with her Dom? And yet here it is, plain as day."

I gulp.

"This is what we're going to do." He says leaning over the desk. "You're going to call your cop mate. Tell him you made a mistake. That there's no missing money. That it's all sorted."

"It was you wasn't it? You stole that money."

He smirks. "Maybe I did Dom, but that's not what these accounts will show…" He slides the paper across. "You see I had enough time to cover my tracks. I couldn't get the cash back but I could at least cover my own ass. Make sure the blame fell on someone else if it came out…"

I stare at it. At the fake transactions. At the paper that makes it look like it was me. "You're setting me up?"

"Only if I have to." He says. "If you play ball, we'll all get what we want, this investigation goes away and you can continue fucking that little whore of a stepdaughter to your hearts content."

I growl getting to my feet.

"Don't be a fool Dom. Don't try and fight this." He says facing me head on. "Besides you don't want anyone else seeing your stepdaughter like this do you?" He says flicking one of the worst photos of her at me. One of the most explicit.

"You really think you'll get away with this?"

"Think of Eden. You want to let everyone in this city know what you've been up to? Let them know what a little slut she is? Do you think our investors will want to keep their money in a business when the CEO behaves like that?"

Maybe I'm stunned into silence because I don't know how to reply. All I know is one way or another I'm going to kill him, I'm going to fucking kill Timothy.

My phone rings. It half screams on the desk and we both jump staring at it for a few moments.

"Aren't you going to get that mate?" Tim says.

I shake my head at him but reach over anyway picking it up.

"Mr Mathers?" A female voice says.

"Who is this?" I half growl taking out my anger and my frustration on the caller.

"It's Katie, Eden's friend. There's, there's been an accident. A, a car crash, Eden.."

"Where is she? Is she okay?"

"She's at the hospital. We're both here."

"Tell her I'm coming. Tell her I'm coming right now." I half-shout before hanging up.

"Trouble in paradise?" Timothy says.

"Fuck you." I say grabbing my keys half running for the door.

"Just remember our bargain. You keep up your end Dom and you can continue getting your cock sucked as much as you want."

I slam the door shut in his god damn face.

I haven't agreed to anything. There's no way in hell I'll agree to it but Christ I won't let him hurt Eden. I won't let him expose her like this.

I guess in a way I've just bought myself a little thinking time and right now I need to focus on Eden. On making sure she's okay. That she's not seriously hurt.

And then I'll deal with Timothy.

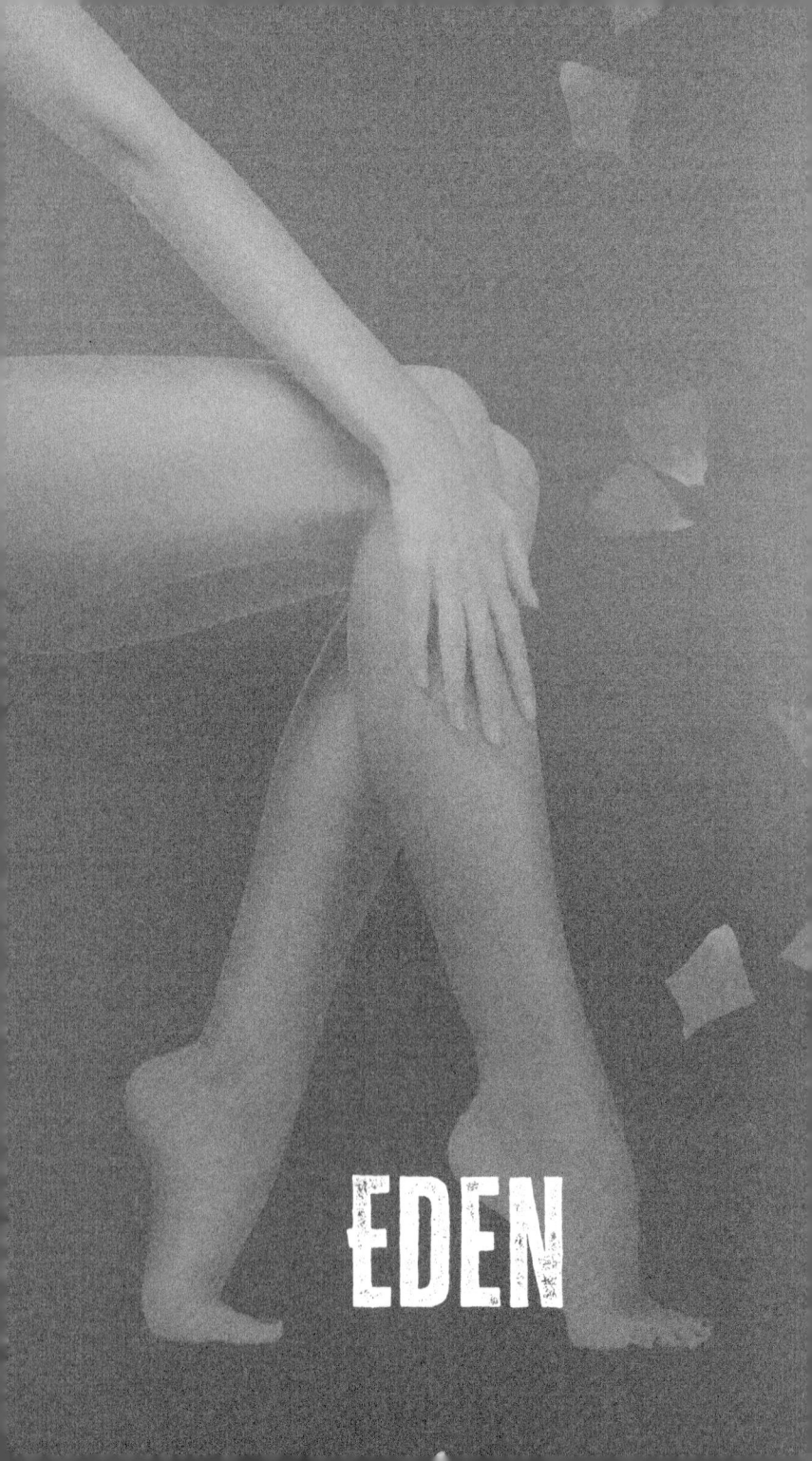

EDEN

Forty-Five

I'm sat in the accident and emergency department.

They've put my left wrist into a cast and given me some painkillers which are thankfully taking the edge off it.

I guess I should be grateful that I'm not more injured. Grateful that I'm even alive.

Katie's beside me. They checked her over but apart from an airbag burn to her face she doesn't have any other injuries.

"I called your stepdad." She says. "I hope you don't mind but I didn't want to call your mum."

"That's okay." I say. I'd rather she called Dominic because right now he's the only person I want to see. In truth the only person I need.

As if by perfect timing I see him walking in, looking flustered, and the nurse points across to me.

I feel my breath catch in my throat as my eyes meet his.

"Eden." I see him mouth but he's half running to me, wrapping his arms around me and I bury my face in his chest. I don't care who sees. I don't care what they think either.

"You came." I murmur breathing in his scent. Feeling the strength of him as he holds me and in this moment he feels so incredibly safe.

"Of course I did." He says pulling away, cupping my face and a part of me wants him to kiss me right now.

Katie clears her throat and I glance at her. She's giving me a look. A curious look. That I have to try so hard not to blush at.

"Are you hurt?" Dominic asks and I turn my eyes back to him.

"Only my wrist." I say holding it up.

"Is it broken?"

I nod. "It's a small break though. A hairline fracture they called it."

He shakes his head. "What happened?"

"Some idiot jumped the lights." I say.

"That idiot to be precise." Katie adds nodding her head in the direction of the man only a few beds over. From what I can tell he got off lightly, only a mild concussion.

"Him?" He says to her and she nods.

Suddenly Dominic's crossing the space, grabbing him, half hauling him out by the scruff of his neck.

"You piece of shit." Dominic growls.

"Dominic." I cry.

"Do you know what you did? You almost killed her." He shouts.

The man splutters. He's clearly high as a kite and his body movements are all off. It's a wonder the police haven't arrived yet.

"Dominic." I say louder.

The nurses are trying to pull him off. I jump from the bed, my heart is thumping so loudly.

"Stop." I say putting my hands on him. "I'm okay. I'm not hurt."

He looks at me. "He broke your wrist. He could have killed you."

"But he didn't." I say.

He shakes his head dropping the man so that he falls back against the bed.

"It's okay." I say to Dominic because I can see he's still raging.

"No it's not." He replies wrapping his arm around me and leading me away.

Katie's staring open-mouthed again. I drop my gaze. I can't look at her right now because then she'll know. She'll see it in my face.

"Is she okay to be discharged?" Dominic asks as the doctor appears.

"I'll just sort the paperwork now."

"Good." He says and then he turns to me. "Let's get you home."

"What about Katie?"

"Are your parents picking you up?" He asks her.

Katie shakes her head. "They're out of town."

"Can we give her a lift?" I ask. I'm not going to let her get a taxi home. I want to make sure she's back safe. It's only fair. And besides she'd do the same for me.

"Sure." He says. "Let's go."

DOMINIC

Forty-Six

Once we've dropped her friend back I drive us home. I messaged Terri because I could hardly not seeing as she's Eden's mum. Only she's too busy in a meeting to come home and check on her only daughter. I guess I shouldn't even be surprised by it now but I am.

We pull up outside and I get out going round to open the door for her.

"I can do it myself." She half laughs.

"I know but…" I begin before sighing and getting the front door.

She walks in behind me and drops her bag. Milton comes running up to her yapping and she smiles picking him up and nuzzling into his face.

"My car's a write-off." She states.

"I'll buy you another one." I say. "Whatever car you want."

"That's silly. I've got some money saved anyway, and with the insurance I'm sure I'll get something decent."

"No." I reply. "I'll not have you drive some clapped out rust bucket. I want you in the safest car possible."

"Dominic…"

I narrow my eyes. I know I'm being all alpha male right now but I can't help it. I take Milton and put him on the floor and then pull her into my arms. "I'm not risking your life."

"It wasn't that bad." She says.

"I don't care."

She's trembling I realise. Her whole body is shaking.

"Nothing's going to happen to you. I won't let anything happen to you." I state.

She nods. "I'm tired."

"Why don't you go lie down. Get some rest. You'll feel better for it."

"Stay with me?"

I sigh. I want too. Hell I want that more than anything. But if Terri comes back? I look down at her face.

I can't do it, I can't leave her alone after this. I won't either.

"I'll be along in a moment. I'll make you a drink in case you get thirsty."

She smiles weakly and walks away. And I stand watching as she goes.

If Terri catches us now then so be it. If it all crumbles I'll take that, I'll take our complete and utter downfall if that's the consequence of comforting her right now.

I grab a glass filling it with water and make my way through the house.

She's already in bed by the time I get there. Milton is on the floor by her feet, chewing on a toy she's no doubt bought him. I put the glass down on the bedside cabinet and watch her for a moment.

I can't really explain what I'm thinking with everything that's happened in the last few hours. The fact that it's Timothy behind it all, the fact that he's been watching us, watching her.

Right now I don't even care about my business, about the money, about the fact that Timothy's blackmailing me, about if this gets out it'll ruin me, because all I can think about is her, Eden. How I could have lost her today and how all of this, this relationship or whatever the hell it is means more to me than anything else in my life.

"Aren't you getting in?" She asks. She's watching me nervously, as if she doesn't understand my behaviour.

"Do you want me to?"

"Yes."

I pull my clothes off quickly, dump them on the floor and clamber in beside her. As she snuggles in against me I can feel she's naked too.

She lets out a little moan that sounds like she's content and I kiss her head.

"I was so scared for a minute." She half whispers. "I saw that car coming at us and I thought that was it. I thought I'd die and I'd never see you again."

"You're safe now."

She turns in my arms to face me. "I love you Dominic. Not the way I should. Not because you're my stepdad. I love you like I've never loved anyone. And I'm so afraid that I'll lose you."

"You won't. I'm not going anywhere. I promise you Eden." I half growl. And then I admit it, what I've been feeling, hell what I've know from the very beginning if I'm honest.

"I love you too. I love you so much. I don't care how wrong this is. I don't care what anyone else thinks or says. I love you and I want to be with you."

She's kissing me, her mouth, her soft lips are against me and her body is writhing. Maybe I should just leave it at this but right now I want more, I need more, and I swear she does too.

I grab her leg bending it up at an angle and slide into her.

"Oh fuck." She gasps.

"I love you Eden." I say as I start thrusting into her, as I kiss her arm, her shoulder, her neck and then her mouth.

She moans, she gyrates, her beautiful body melds with mine and for a few moments it's like nothing else exists but us, lost in our ecstasy, our own damnation too. And then she's clawing at me, gasping, dragging her nails down my skin as she gets closer and closer to her climax.

"That's it Eden." I groan as her walls grip my cock so deliciously it hurts. "Cum for me."

"Dominic." She gasps. "Oh fuck Dominic." She screams the last word. My name. She screams my name and in answer I reach my own orgasm.

EDEN

Forty-Seven

He loves me. He said it.

I keep hearing the words in my head. Repeating them.

Maybe we're both mad. Maybe we're both crazy but there's a part of me that believes we could actually get what we want. That my mother will go and me and Dominic will live together, be together, have our happy ending.

I sigh, leaning into him. He's holding me still. I can hear his breathing, I can feel it on my skin.

My wrist hurts just enough to have woken me and I have no idea what time it is, I only know that it's late, or early depending on how you look at it.

I turn to watch him for a moment.

My stepdad. A man twenty something years older than me. A man I should never have looked at and wanted and yet from the minute I glanced up and saw him watching me it was like something in me clicked. Some lost part of myself came back.

I can't exist without him. I can't be me without him.

He's the other part of me, he understands me, he gets me, he makes me feel in a way nobody else has ever even realised existed.

He doesn't look at me like I'm a child, like I'm an idiot. He doesn't treat me like I'm anything less than him, he acts like I'm his equal. He listens to me, he laughs at my jokes, he's interested in what I have to say and for the first time in my life I feel valued for who I am, not what I am.

He groans in his sleep and I stifle a giggle. He's dreaming.

I could wake him up, I could make him entertain me while I'm here with my mind going into overdrive but I won't. I sink into the pillows pulling Milton into my arms willing myself to sleep and I hope that while I am I dream of him.

Of Dominic.

DOMINIC

Forty-Eight

I wake and she's sound asleep. I wonder if her wrist woke her up during the night because usually she's awake well before me.

For a moment I watch her. She looks so fragile and yet so strong all in one. As if that's possible.

She's so beautiful. Her hair is all tussled. Her face looks so peaceful. Her arms are tightly wrapped around the puppy and he's soundo too. The two of them make a fine pair.

For a moment I can see it, the two of us living together openly, free of the lies and the deceit. I see Milton, fully grown, lying at our feet as we cuddle or watch a movie or just simply enjoy each other's company and I see a baby too, our baby. Mine and Eden's. God am I mad to want that? To hope for that? To believe that in this world, with everything stacked against us, that we could ever achieve that kind of peace?

I get up, more because my head is spinning and I don't want to disturb her. And anyway I need some thinking space about the whole Timothy situation. I need to figure this out and I need to come up with a plan because no way am I taking the fall for this and no way in hell is he getting away with this either.

I pull on my clothes. Somewhere in the house Terri could be lurking and I don't want to do anything that rocks the boat right now. That puts Eden in the firing range. She's my first priority and I will do everything necessary to protect her.

As I walk back through the hallway I freeze. Terri is there staring at me.

"Why were you in her room?" She says.

"What?"

"Why were you in Eden's room? That's where you just came from."

"I was checking on her." I say. "You know, after the car crash."

She sighs. "How is she?"

"She's alive." I half growl.

"Dom…"

"Don't Terri." I snap. "She's your daughter and you couldn't even be bothered to come back home and see her. She could have died."

"I wanted to. I tried."

"Clearly not hard enough." I state walking away.

I don't have time to think about Terri right now, I've got bigger fish to fry. Far bigger fish.

I jump in the shower, get dressed and drive to the train station. I need to see Bob. In person. It's the only logical move. To lay all my cards in front of Bob and see what he can do.

But Jesus is it going to be a painful conversation.

When I get to Scotland Yard I have to sit and wait for someone to come out with a visitor badge. Maybe I should have called ahead but I wasn't sure how to even broach the situation and it felt easier to just focus on the here and now, take each step at a time. Get to the station first. Then go from there.

They lead me into an interview room. Bob comes in with woman he introduces as his SIC, Cara Franks.

They sit opposite me. It feels like an interrogation but I guess with everything I'm about to say that's exactly what this could turn into.

"Interview beginning at 11.37am with Dominic Mathers. Officers in attendance Chief Inspector Bob Aldross and Detective Sergeant Cara Franks." Cara says after the machine lets out a long almost irritating buzz.

"So Dominic, you say you have new information on this fraud case." Bob says.

"I do." I reply. "I know who is taking the money. It's my Finance Director Timothy Grice."

"And what makes you say that?" Cara asks.

"Because he's trying to blackmail me." I state. "He came into my office. He said he's fixed the accounts so it looks as though I'm behind it. He said he wanted me to call you lot and tell you it's all a mistake. That there is no fraud. But if you don't take the bait then I'm the one who's supposed to take the fall."

And then Bob asks the million dollar question. The one thing I know I have to be truthful about but the one thing in all of this I am so desperate to keep to myself.

"What's he blackmailing you about?"

I draw in a deep breath. Clench and unclench my fists.

I could lie. I could deny it. Hell, I don't even have to tell them. They only need to know that I'm being blackmailed, they don't need to know the grisly details and yet in this moment I feel like saying it out loud protects her too, that somehow this will keep her safe, as illogical as it sounds in my own head.

"I'm having an affair." I state.

"With..?"

"My stepdaughter."

"What?" Bob says his eyes snapping to me. Christ he thinks I'm a pervert. A paedophile even.

"She's not underage." I say quickly. "She's an adult. We're both adults."

I can feel the way they're looking at me. Judging me. Bob is so black and white, so straight and narrow that I bet the thought of me doing anything like this never even entered his mind.

"I see." He says, narrowing his eyes. He thinks I'm an arsehole. He thinks I'm a sick bastard. I guess in a way he's right. I am all of those things.

"What's your stepdaughter's name? For the records." Cara says.

"Eden." I state. "Eden Mathers. She has the same surname as me. I married her mother eight years ago."

Jesus why did I have to say that bit? Who gives a shit when I married Terri? No one was even asking that.

"Does Eden know about any of this?" Bob asks.

"No. She's got nothing to do with this. Beyond being the source of the blackmail."

He nods.

"Look, I will do whatever you want." I growl. "I will wear a wire, I will let you look through all my own personal accounts. I didn't take this money and I sure as hell am not going to be the fall guy."

Bob sits back in his chair, folding his arms. Assessing me.

"Alright Dominic. This is what we're going to do. We're going to look into this Timothy chap. We'll do some recon. Pulls what accounts we can find. I assume you agreed to his demands?"

"I haven't agreed to anything. Eden was in a car crash. I walked out on Timothy because I had to get to the hospital."

"Is she okay?" Cara asks but it sounds more like she's being polite than anything else.

"She's got a broken wrist. Some arsehole jumped the red lights and crashed right into her car." I state.

"So you've not said yes to him?" Bob confirms.

"No."

"Then perhaps we have an opportunity here." He says. "Because if what you're saying is true, I doubt he will leave it hanging. He'll want to be sure in his own head that he's silenced you."

"What do you want me to do?" I ask.

"We'll get some camera's set up. Covert. In your office. All you have to do is get him to admit it, to talk about the fact he's behind it, hell, get him to blackmail you again."

"Fine." I agree. "How soon can we move on this?"

"We can get some hidden camera's installed today assuming the CPS give authorisation." Cara says more to Bob than me. "I'll speak to the local team as soon as we're done here."

He nods looking at her before looking back at me.

"It might be best if you avoid the office until we're all set. We don't want to miss the boat." Bob says and I grunt in agreement. He's right. Better I stay in the city for a night. Head back tomorrow and then face Timothy with everything in place for his just deserts.

EDEN

Forty-Nine

Dominic had to go to London for some big meeting. I wanted to go join him. I even asked to travel up and spend the night despite the fact I knew he'd say no. He's right, it would be too risky, too obvious too.

He left yesterday and I threw my head into updating this damn dissertation because it felt like an appropriate way to channel my feelings, only it's hard to type with just one properly functioning hand.

I'm frustrated, angry, resentful even. Mum is making a big point of being in the house, of rearranging things, nesting almost as if she's trying to reclaim this space. I wonder if on some level she's aware of what's happened, as if subconsciously she senses the betrayal.

She hasn't even asked how my wrist is and yet she comments about the missing sofa in the orangery. The one I ruined when I squirted all over Dominic's face. It's so hard not to blush. I tell her Dominic spilt some red wine and we couldn't get it out. That a new one's on order.

And then I get the hell out. I can't be around her. I feel guilty at not feeling guilty. I feel bitter at her presence and in truth I don't really like myself very much right now. I'm the other woman. I'm the whore stealing her husband and though she's not exactly a saint herself what with her own affair, two wrongs don't make a right.

We're both bad people. Maybe that's what we have in common. That's what I inherited from her.

I message Dominic and he says he's on the train back so I decide to grab a taxi to his office and meet him as a nice surprise.

He's not there when I turn up and his secretary says I can wait for him but she's leaving early for some dental appointment. Is it wrong that I see the positives in that? That at least she won't be sat outside if things get a little physical?

I sit on the couch, pulling out a reference book I found earlier to try and distract myself. I can't decide whether it helps or hinders my argument. I'm flicking through the pages, trying to find something, anything of actual use when the door opens and I grin looking up.

Only it's not Dominic. It's Timothy.

My face falls.

"Hello Eden. What are you doing here?" Even his voice sets me on edge now.

"Waiting for Dominic."

He smirks like there's some big joke going on. "Of course you are." He mutters shutting the door.

"Why are you here?" I ask back.

"Well I would have said the same thing but now you're here…" He's grinning.

"What does that mean?" I ask.

He crosses the room and sits right by me. Staring at me.

"You know considering what you did back at the party I think I'd prefer if you waited outside." I state.

"Oh would you now?" He says taking the book from my lap and tossing it onto the table with a loud thump that makes me jump.

"You know what, I'll just wait outside then." I say getting up only he grabs my arm yanking it hard, yanking me hard and I half stumble back into him.

"Not this time you Eden." He says.

"Let go of me." I snap.

He laughs. "You can stop pretending now."

"Pretending what?"

"That you're not a little cockslut."

"What?"

"Or is it just Dom's cock you've got a taste for? Because I know what the pair of you have been up to."

I shake my head. I'm not going to admit it and especially not to him. I push him off, but I only get just beyond the couch before he's grabbing me again.

"Here's how this is gonna go, you're gonna play nice, give me a little piece of what Dominic is having and maybe I might keep it from your mum."

"Fuck you." I say before spitting in his face.

He screws his face up, wiping the saliva off and then he hits me, right across the cheekbone and I fall back hard into the desk, smashing my bad wrist against it and it screams in protest.

He moves quickly, pushing me further into it and wrenching my good arm behind my back to an almost impossible angle. It doesn't help that my other wrist is practically useless with the cast on it.

"You're hurting me." I cry.

He lets out a little laugh. "Don't worry Eden, I'll make you feel real good in a minute."

He's got his whole weight on me, holding me down now as he yanks my leggings and thong down, pulling them right over my ass and hips. I try to kick out but my clothes are now acting like restraints stifling my movements. I try to get free and he slams my face into the wood, compounding the bruise he's already given me.

"Stop fighting me." He says.

"Get off me." I cry. "Please."

"I'm sure you'll love my cock as much as you do Dom's, you dirty little slut."

I scream back. I can't stop screaming.

"I'll give you something to scream about Eden." He says, unzipping his trousers and my panic increases tenfold as I feel his erection against me. "You'll be screaming loud enough when you cum on my cock."

And then the door swings open and Dominic's stood there.

I swear time stands still for a second. He's staring right at me. At Timothy too as he's holding me down with his dick half out of his trousers.

"Get the fuck off her." Dominic growls before crossing the room, grabbing him, and slamming him into the wall.

I sink down off the desk, pulling my leggings back up, covering myself. My shoulder is aching from how he held my arm and my face is throbbing from where he hit me.

Dominic is laying punches into him. One after another. I think he might kill him. Might just beat him to death.

"Dominic." I half whisper and he stops, turning to look at me.

His face is all fury, all rage, but when his eyes meet mine they soften.

"Come here." He says moving to me and he picks me up, cradling me in his arms.

I bury my face in his chest. I feel dirty, ashamed, but now that Dominic is here, I finally feel safe too.

He carries me out of the room, puts me on the couch just outside and shuts the door to his office leaving Timothy in whatever state he is in. And then he wraps his arms around me as he pulls out his phone and makes a call.

"Hi Bob." He says. "No, that's not going to happen now."

The man on the other end says something.

"No." Dominic replies. "Timothy just tried to rape Eden."

I gulp at the word. I know that's what was happening but to hear it spoken out loud makes it so much worse.

They talk a little more but I'm already zoning out, mentally disassociating I guess. My adrenaline is coursing through me and it's all I can do not to puke.

When he hangs up, he stays where he is, holding me, cradling me, until the Police arrive and they take Timothy into custody and us both in for questioning.

DOMINIC

Fifty

They separated us at the station.

I know it makes sense, we can hardly be interviewed together, but I keep wondering where she is and how she's coping.

I've got a pack of ice on my knuckles. I half expect someone to mention charges for ABH but they're not, and I wonder if it's because they'd all do the same if they were in my position.

Bob arrives a few hours later. He immediately sits down with the detectives interviewing me.

They've got it all on tape. I guess I should be grateful that they put the surveillance cameras up straight away but the thought that anyone has seen what happened, seen Eden in that moment, makes me so fucking angry.

"How is she?" I ask for what must be the hundredth time.

"She's with specially trained officers." Bob says echoing the same words the others have each time they reply.

I sigh shaking my head.

"The good news is we can link the money to him." Bob says and I look back at him.

"How?"

"He's not as clever as he thinks. You can't just wire money and think there's no trace. While the paperwork might point to you we can prove you're not the one who's done it."

"So I'm in the clear?" I ask.

"Yes Dom. But it'll be a messy fight at court. We'll need you to give evidence."

"I'll do whatever is necessary." I state.

"And Eden?" Bob says.

I wince. Christ, how did I get her caught up in all this? "It's her decision. I won't make her do anything she doesn't want to."

All three of them nod.

"Do you know why he did it?" It's not like he's strapped for cash. He's got enough shares in the business, he's got a plush house, hell even his salary matches mine and Eric's.

"He's got debts."

"What debts?" I ask screwing my face up.

"Gambling debts. From what we can tell he frittered it all away. Kept chasing the big win that would save his ass. Only it never came."

"Fuck." I mutter. I knew he liked the slots. I saw him playing on his phone often enough but I didn't realise it was to that extent. I thought it was a bit of fun. Not something serious and certainly not an addiction.

Someone taps on the door before sticking their head round. It's a woman, in her forties, she glances at me before looking at the detectives. "We're done." She says. Bob nods.

"So are we." The detective beside him says and the woman opens the door so we can all see Eden stood, arms around herself avoiding everyone's gaze.

"Eden." I murmur getting up and walking to her.

She looks up and gives me a weak smile. "I'm okay." She says. But she's not. I can see she's not.

"Shall we go home?" I say gently.

"Yeah." She says leaning into me and I wrap my arms around her, holding her so tightly, and kiss her head.

I don't care who sees.

I don't care who knows because let's face it they all do.

In this moment I just care about her and I need her to know that.

EDEN

Fifty-One

They separated us. I kept asking for him and they kept saying that he was with other officers and would be free soon.

Only he's not.

I huddle in the chair. They're looking at me like I deserve sympathy. Like I'm some sort of victim.

I guess in a way I am.

I gulp looking away. I think I'm going to be sick. I think I'm going to puke.

I can barely get the words out before I'm running for the door but there's nowhere to go. I don't even know where the toilets are and I heave in the hallway, puking my guts up, as one of them comes up behind saying something meant to be comforting.

And then she touches me.

I know it's meant to be reassuring but it isn't. I cry out, jerking away and almost fall into my own sick patch.

"Come and sit down." The other one says. "We'll get you some water."

I nod, it's not like I have a choice is it?

I sink back in the chair and they put a plastic cup in front of me. I stare at it. At the water rocking slightly inside before it comes to a standstill.

"Eden…" One of them says gently.

"What?" I ask.

"Can we talk about what happened?"

I shake my head. I don't want to talk about it. I don't even want to think about it. All I want right now is Dominic and they're keeping me from him.

I ask for him again and they just give me the same response.

And then they try another tactic. "Do you know about the blackmail?"

I frown looking up. "What blackmail?"

"Timothy was blackmailing Dominic." The woman says, Sandra is her name. I don't know why I remember it at this moment but I do.

"About what?" I say and then I gulp. "About me?"

They exchange glances. Of course it was.

"He had pictures. Photos of the two of you." Sandra continues.

"What photos?" I say.

The other one, the taller one lays them out and I gasp. Jesus fucking Christ. He had photos of us? Of me? I shut my eyes looking away. That prick took photos. He stalked us? He saw me like that. If I hadn't just have puked I think I might be throwing up again.

"Eden I understand this is hard."

"Do you?" I snarl. I don't mean to take my anger out on her but right now it's the only way to deal with this.

"Do you know about the money?"

"What money?" I say glaring at them.

Again they exchange glances but clearly there's something going on over my head.

"He tried to rape me." I say and they look at me then. Properly.

"Can you talk us through what happened?" Sandra says.

I clench my jaw, take a sip of my water and then stare at the table. "I was waiting for Dominic to get back. He walked in. He grabbed me. He said if I didn't want him to tell my mum about Dominic and I that I…" I shake my head. I can't get the words out. I can't even say it.

God I wasn't even raped, what the fuck is wrong with me?

"It's okay. Take your time." Tall lady says.

"He grabbed me, he pinned me against the desk and he half stripped me."

"Did he penetrate you?"

I jerk then. "Why the fuck does that matter?" I snarl.

"I'm not meaning to be insensitive here, but this is the difference between rape and attempted rape." She says and I get it then. They're trying to figure out what to charge him with.

"He didn't." I say. "Dominic stopped him before he could."

They ask me more questions then. And I become a robot, answering them as if none of it matters. As if I don't even have feelings anymore.

"Will there be a trial?" I ask. They exchange glances. "He's not getting off, surely?"

"He isn't." Sandra says. "We have enough evidence to charge him."

"So I'll need to give evidence at court?"

"Potentially. If he decides to plead not guilty." Tall lady says. "We have some footage of the attack so it may be he decides to own up to it."

"Excuse me?" I say frowning.

"Our colleagues had hidden cameras in the room. It was for a different reason but it got everything that happened." Sandra says.

"So you didn't even need to ask me then?" I snarl. "You have it all on tape? Why the fuck did I even have to explain it?"

"We needed your account of what happened." Sandra says. "I'm sorry. This is never easy."

I shake my head. Feeling my anger flash again. "Are we done here?"

They sigh. "Yes." Sandra says. "Let's leave it there."

I get up, half jump from my seat. "Where's Dominic?"

"I can take you to him if you want."

"That's all I wanted. From the minute you brought me in here." I say back.

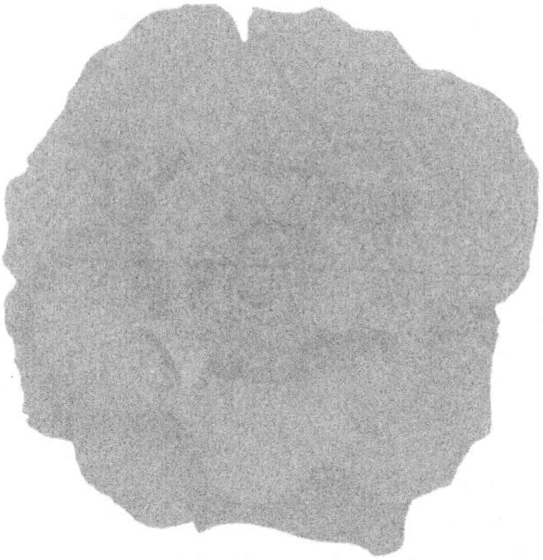

DOMINIC

Fifty-Two

When we get home she scoops Milton into her arms and says she wants to be alone. That she wants a little space to think and clear her head.

I watch her go and my heart sinks because I caused this. I hired Timothy years ago, I was the one who brought that man into her life. Hell, if I'd not been messing with her, none of this would have happened.

I want to hug her, I want to wrap my arms around her and tell her she's safe, that it's all over but I feel like right now that's too much.

I sit up late into the night, I sit in my office brooding. Thinking it over, trying to pin point when exactly I should have realised who Tim really was. What more I could have done to protect her from him.

I don't know what time I hear the door open and I sigh, ready for another confrontation with Terri. She must have seen the light on, god I hope she's not going to try anything because I don't have the patience for it. And I don't have the energy for another fight either.

I turn ready to tell her where she can go.

Only it's not her.

It's Eden.

I frown staring at her. She's got her arms wrapped around her, she's wearing a big baggy hoody, and she's staring right back at me.

"Why are you still up?" She asks.

"I couldn't sleep." I say.

She lets out a little exhale of air. "Me neither."

"Eden." I murmur and then clear my throat. "I'm so sorry. I had no idea who he was, what he was capable of."

"It's not for you to apologise." She says. "You didn't do this and besides I should have spoken up the first time."

I frown. "What?"

She drops her gaze stepping up to the window and stares out at where the spotlights highlight the trees at the bottom of the garden by the hot tub.

"He tried it before." She says.

"Excuse me?"

She flinches at the tone and I internally berate myself for scaring her.

"When did he try it before?" I ask as gently as I can.

"Months ago. When we had that party here. He got into the hot tub with me. He tried it on, he called me a slut."

I narrow my eyes remembering back to it. She'd called herself a slut that day too if I recall it right. "That was why you were upset when you came back into the house."

She nods.

"Why didn't you say anything then?" I ask.

She looks at me and gives a little laugh. "I told him where to stick it. I thought it would be enough, that he'd take the hint."

"But you didn't tell me."

"I didn't think you'd have believed me." She murmurs.

"Eden."

"It's okay, if I'm honest I sort of just brushed it off. We were starting whatever we were and my focus was on that. Not him."

I pull her into my arms, half expecting her to push me off, to not want to be touched right now, but she leans in, almost welcoming it.

"He was blackmailing you." She says.

"Yes."

"He had photos of us."

"I don't know how he got those…"

"He was watching us." She says and I hear the anger then. She's right to be angry, she's right to be fucking furious.

"He's going to go away for a long time." I state. "He'll never get near you again."

She nods, burying her face into my chest and I wrap my arms around her head. She feels like she's trembling, heaving, and I realise that she's crying, silently sobbing against my shirt.

"Eden. I'm so sorry."

She doesn't reply. She just keeps crying and I keep holding her, hoping that my presence, my arms, hell that all of me is comforting her enough.

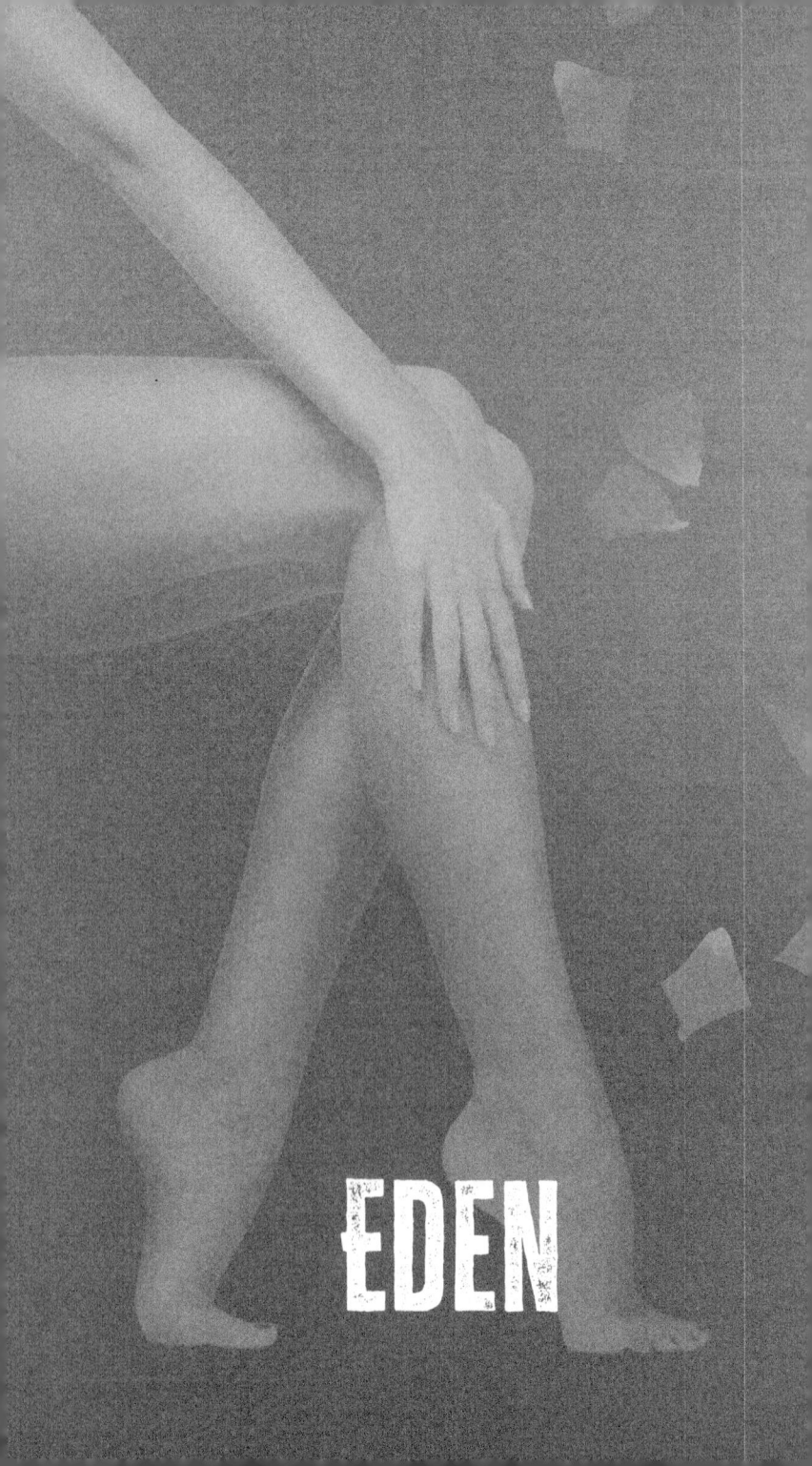

EDEN

Fifty-Three

I'm sat in a lecture. I know I could have gotten out of it but I need the distraction. After everything that happened yesterday the thought of sitting around the house, of dwelling on it, of even seeing the places that Timothy could have been lurking in, is enough to force me to college.

Only it feels like everyone keeps staring at me.

I've got a bruise across my face where Timothy hit me and then slammed my head into the desk. I've covered as best I can with makeup but it still shows through anyway. I guess I should be grateful those are the only injuries I sustained but I don't feel all the grateful right now.

I'm half tempted to pull up the hoody I've got on and hide but I know my professor will only call me out because he hates people sat with beanies, baseball caps, anything like that. It's unprofessional in his eyes. Disrespectful too.

When the lecture's finally done I head out to find Katie. Normally we meet for a coffee on Thursdays as we both finish at the same time and by god could I use one now.

I head up through the library and more people are looking. I frown because I doubt my face is that bad. And anyway they're being so blatant about it. So god damn obvious.

"Eden." Katie says looking half like she's seen a ghost when I sink down into the chair beside her.

"It's a long story." I mutter. And one I'm not quite ready to talk about.

"What is?" She says confused.

"The bruise." I state. What else does she think I mean?

"Eden, have you checked your phone today? Or social media? Or anything?" She asks.

"No why?" I say pulling my phone from my bag. I've been too distracted to look at it but as I look at the screen there's dozens of messages, missed calls, notifications. It's like my phone's been having a party for the entire day in my bag. God it's a good thing I had it on silent or my professors would have lost their head at me.

"Eden, everyone knows." She says.

"Knows what?" I ask.

She pushes a newspaper to me. "You're fucking Dominic. You're fucking your stepdad."

My eyes nearly pop out of my head as I take in the headline and the photo of Dominic and my mother from last year's Gala. *'Mathers Brother In Family Sleaze Scandal.'* It's a local paper. But it's front page news. We are front page news.

I grab it scanning the paragraphs. It's all about us. About me and Dominic. I wrench the paper open and inside there's a blurred out photo of me, in my underwear, with Dominic and it's more than obvious what we're about to get up to.

Jesus fucking Christ.

"I…" I look up at Katie just as my phone rings.

"Dominic?" I say picking it up.

"I've been trying to get hold of you for hours. Where are you?" He asks.

"In, in the library." I murmur.

"You need to go home. Right now. The papers have got the story. They've run with it."

"I know." I say. "It's on the front page. There's pictures of us."

"I think Timothy did it. He must have done it while we were waiting for the Police to show. One final fuck you I guess."

I can't help it, I look up and it feels like everyone is staring. "Dominic everyone knows." I half whisper.

"Get home Eden. Get a taxi if you have too. Just get home." Dominic says.

"You're fucking Dominic?" Katie says as soon as I put the phone down.

"Katie…"

"Why didn't you tell me?" She says looking hurt.

"I…" I shake my head. God I don't think I can take anymore drama right now. "Do you have your car? Can you drive me home?"

"Yeah I can." Katie says grabbing her bag. "Let's go."

We rush out the door and she half hisses at the people who are muttering, staring, half gawping at me.

When I get in the passenger side she's already in, seat belt on, half grinning.

"What is so funny?" I ask.

"You're fucking Dominic?" She says. "Dominic?"

"It's complicated."

"Sure it is." She says turning the engine on. "You're into older men."

I burst out laughing. "Not exactly."

"Tell me the details."

"That's your response?" I reply. I thought she was going to be angry. I thought she was going to tell me what an idiot I've been.

"Can you at least tell me what he's like in bed? I mean does experience really make a difference or is it the same as being with someone our age?"

"I wouldn't know." I say meeting her eyes. "I've only ever been with Dominic."

Her jaw drops. "You, you…" She starts giggling. "Jesus Eden that's so wrong."

"What is?" I say.

"You gave your virginity to your stepdad?"

I laugh, folding my arms as best I can with my wrist still in the cast, watching the traffic as we drive. Yeah it is wrong but even now, even when the world is crashing around me, I wouldn't change it.

"Oh my god, that's why he had you on a curfew, you were fucking while your mum was away." She says and I blush then.

"Fuck Eden." She says before laughing. "You made it sound like he was being a prick but really you were going home each day to ride his dick."

"Oh my god can you stop?" I say half laughing as well.

We fall silent and she turns back to focusing on the road again.

"I love him Katie." I say.

"Like a stepdad or a boyfriend?" She asks.

I look at her properly. "I love him."

"Does he love you?"

"He says he does." I state.

"God I wish I had your life."

"Excuse me?"

"Come on you've got to admit how hot this is."

I shake my head. "I'll remind you of that when I'm a complete pariah."

She smirks. "Nah you won't be. You just need to make sure he kicks your mum out and upgrades you to his master suite."

"Fucking hell." I laugh as we pull up outside the gates.

"Keep me updated. I want to know everything. And I mean everything."

"Goodbye Katie." I say grinning as I shut the door. It's not funny. It shouldn't be funny. Christ this is the worst possible outcome from all of this and yet the fact my best friend is supporting me makes me feel a little better.

I unlock the side gate and make my way through to the main house.

And then my heart literally stops when I see my mum's home. Jesus this is going to be one hell of a conversation now. I'm half tempted to turn around, to hide out somewhere until Dominic gets back but where can I go? It feels like the entire city knows what I've done. I can hardly sit in a café while I'm openly discussed as the whore of the century.

So I grit my teeth and pray to god I can sneak into my room unnoticed. Hide out with Milton until it's safe.

Only she's there, carrying a suitcase down the stairs. Her face falls slightly when she sees me.

"Eden." She says.

"Mum."

"Go get your things, get packing."

"What?" I frown. The fuck is she talking about?

"Everyone knows Eden."

"I know everyone knows." I snap back. Though why the hell she's not screaming bloody murder at me I don't know.

"What do you think Dominic will do when he gets home? Do you think he'll still let us stay here?" She cries.

"What are you talking about?"

"My affair. The papers have it as headline news." She hisses dumping the bag and crossing to where she's left a tabloid and she picks it up waving it about.

"You haven't read it have you?" I say.

"Of course I haven't. I know the actual details so why do I need to read what they're calling me?"

I gulp. Oh shit. She thinks it's about her. I could almost laugh in this moment at the absurdity of this.

"I'm pregnant Eden." She says.

"What?"

"I'm pregnant. It's Colin's."

"You, you can even get pregnant?" I don't mean to be nasty it's just I thought women her age had hit the menopause already. I guess I'm wrong.

"I'm thirty nine. I'm not a geriatric." She hisses.

"Alright." I reply. "So let me get this straight, you're pregnant with Colin's baby and you what, think that I'm just going to go with you?"

"Where else will you go?" She snaps slamming the paper back down and grabbing her case again. "Dominic won't want you around."

"Is that so?" He says walking in and I feel my body react as he gets closer to me. I can't even help it. It's visceral. It's instinctive.

Mum's face goes pale, paler. "Dominic…."

He looks at the suitcases. "So you're leaving, are you?"

"I think it's best." She says.

"Yeah you're right." He says.

She looks at me again. "Go and pack."

"No." Dominic and I say together.

She turns to glare at him. "What the fuck is this? She's my daughter."

"And some mother you make." He says. "You barely notice she exists except to belittle her. You didn't even check to see if she was alright after that car crash so don't pretend that you care now."

"I was busy."

"Busy fucking your boss." I snap before I can stop myself.

Dominic looks at me with wide eyes.

"Shut up." Mum snaps before looking at Dominic. "She's my daughter. She's coming with me."

"She's not going anywhere." Dominic says and instinctively I step back into him and he wraps his arms around me.

She stares at us dumbfounded. "What is this?" She snarls.

I don't know why he does it, why he chooses that moment, but he kisses my head, in the same reassuring way he did back at the police station.

"You…" She shakes her head slightly. "You.."

I'm not even trembling. I thought I would be. I thought that when this moment came I'd be so scared of her reaction but I realise that I don't care. I don't care what she says. And having Dominic's arms around me makes me feel that there's nothing she can do either.

"You slept with my daughter?" She says. "You, you fucked my daughter?"

Dominic lets out a noise like a growl. It sounds protective, domineering. My heart jumps as he does it and I squeeze his arms as I wrap my hands around them.

"And you." She says pointing her finger at me. "You filthy little whore. Bet you were more than happy to spread your legs, to steal my husband out right from under my nose."

"He's not yours." I snarl before I can stop myself.

"You're disgusting. Both of you." She shouts. "She's a child Dominic. A child. What kind of sick fuck seduces a child?"

"Get out." Dominic says. "Get out of my house."

She shakes her head.

"That's why you were in her room the other day wasn't it? You were fucking her while I was in the house?"

"Get out or I'll throw you out." Dominic says.

She screws her face up, grabbing her suitcases and rolls them behind her, as she half runs from us both.

DOMINIC

Fifty-Four

We're stood, her still in my arms, listening as the sound of her tyres screeching disappears. She's leaning into me with all her weight and I can practically feel her heart as it's pounding in her chest.

"I'm so sorry." I murmur.

"I'm not." She says turning round to face me.

I raise an eyebrow.

"There've been so many secrets." She says. "So many lies. I'm pleased it's finally all out."

"How long have you known she was having an affair?" I ask.

She winces. "A while."

I narrow my eyes. "And yet you said nothing?"

"I didn't…" She screws her face up for a second. "I didn't want to tell you because it felt too manipulative. I knew she was screwing her boss, I found out just before she went away but it felt like if I said something I'd only be doing it to try and separate you. To make you leave her for me."

"Oh Eden." I sigh. How the fuck could she think I'd believe that? That I'd even think she was capable of that?

"There's more." She says.

"What else?"

"She's pregnant."

"Excuse me?"

"She told me, before you came in. It's her bosses. Colin's." She states.

I shake my head. "That fucking bitch." I growl.

"Why are you so angry about that?"

"Because she tried to trick me. She tried it on, she said she wanted us to have a baby."

Her eyes widen. "She tried to sleep with you?"

I nod.

"You think she was going to pass it off as yours?" She asks.

"Don't you?" I half snarl.

She shakes her head. "And she said I was manipulative. What a fucking bitch."

"When did she say that?" I ask.

"All the time." She mutters. "She said I was like my dad, manipulative and a waste of space. But it doesn't matter now."

"No it doesn't." I say pulling her back into my arms. "She's gone and she won't be coming back."

"And everyone knows." She whispers.

I lift her face up from under her chin. "At least we no longer have to hide it."

She laughs. "Yeah that's true. We can be us now. We can be together, we can…" She hesitates.

"Can what Eden?"

"Get married. I mean not now, not straight away but…"

"Eden." I say. Sure we're technically now free to do what we want but it doesn't change the fact that I'm way older than her.

"I want to marry you Dominic." She says looking so fierce as she does. "I want to spend the rest of my life with you."

"You say that now, but sweetheart, you might change your mind. You're still young."

She shakes her head. "I know what I want and besides everyone marries with the belief they'll be together forever but no one knows what they'll feel in the future. How their feelings might change. You're making an unfair assumption about me based purely on my age but you could change your mind, in ten years' time you might decide I'm not who you want anymore."

I smirk. Like the hell that would happen but she's right. As much as she might change her mind there's an equal chance she might not. My little Lolita has perhaps more wisdom than her years.

"I see all those essays you write are rubbing off on you, stating your case like that." I reply.

She rolls her eyes. "Dominic."

"No, listen to me." I say putting my finger over her lips. "I love you Eden. I didn't mean to start this. It was a mistake but by god is it the best mistake of my life and if you want me, if you want to get married, hell if you want me to father your children then I'm there, for every second, every minute you'll give me."

Her eyes widen. "I want you Dominic. I've always wanted you." She half breathes out her reply.

I grab her face, plunging my tongue into her mouth.

My sweet little angel is mine, all mine, and no one now can take her from me.

EDEN

Epilogue

Five years later

It's Dominic's birthday.

We've arranged for a whole bunch of our friends as well as his brother and a few very select family to come out to Italy, to a castle in the mountains, to celebrate. They thought we're just here for an extended birthday party.

Only Dominic and I had a little something extra planned.

Katie knew. As did Eric, because it turns out Dominic can't keep secrets from him.

And when we announced what we were really up to the looks on their faces was priceless.

So now I'm here, in the evening heat of the Italian summer, feeling the nerves starting to set in as Katie chats away. A stylist is doing my hair, and a makeup artist is waiting patiently to put the finishing touches to my face.

Katie's already in her dress, a long flowy thing that I half envy but I wouldn't change my dress for the world.

I had it made especially, it's exactly what I envisioned, exactly what I've dreamed of and when I put it on, when I'm ready to go I can barely get over how I look in the mirror.

Katie hands me a posey of flowers and I smile before we head down the spiral staircase to where everyone is waiting. To where Dominic is waiting.

When I walk out the sun is setting. It's exactly as I imagined it. There are candles lighting the path between all the seats and Dominic is there at the very end smiling at me. He's got more grey hairs now, a few creases from where he smiles too, but if anything they make him more devilishly handsome, more irresistible to me.

For a moment, for the briefest second I can't believe that we're here, that everything worked out the way it has.

We lost a lot of friends from the fall out of the affair. My entire family refuses to acknowledge I even exist but they never really liked me anyway so I guess it's not that much of a loss. Dominic lost one investor but the rest stayed. His returns where too good for them to resist even a sex scandal and it's helped that we've stayed together, that from the offset we were clear about it not just being a fling, that it was real, that our feelings for each other were real too.

As I come to stand beside him I can honestly say I've never loved him more.

"You look so beautiful." He murmurs and I blush.

The man starts talking, going through the legalities. We've opted to have the ceremony as short as possible, no readings, no sermon, just me and him, saying our vows, committing ourselves to one another.

When the ceremony is over Dominic kisses me and he doesn't hold back. Like he doesn't care that everyone is watching and I half gasp as he steals the air from my lungs.

We walk hand in hand through the castle to where they've laid out a feast on a huge veranda overlooking the valley below. The view is breath-taking but it's nothing compared to that of my new husband.

Eric passes us both a glass of champagne, congratulating us, and I take a small sip. It'll be my only glass tonight but I don't mind. It's a sacrifice I'm more than willing to make for the future we want, the future we both, very soon, will have.

Eric didn't approve of us for a long time. He made it clear what he thought in private but he also stood by Dominic publicly and for that I'm grateful.

And now? Now he's accepted it. Now he doesn't even act like he ever had reservations.

Someone calls for a toast and a few people shout 'the happy couple' and then Dominic turns facing me, raising his glass and says so proudly, "To my beautiful wife." And then he kisses me again.

Is it sad that I still get a little buzz every time he does that? It's been years now, you think I would have gotten used to it, but even his touch still sends a thrill through me and every time he kisses me it feels like the first time, when he snuck into my room and we had to be so quiet and yet, it took my breath away all the same.

We sold the old house, Dominic's house, and bought an old grade II listed Tudor mansion. Somehow it felt wrong to continue our relationship in a place connected so much with my mother. And the thought that Timothy had been lurking there too didn't help.

Our new home is beautiful. It's got so much history, so much character, and we've spent ages making it ours. Our home.

We take a seat, Dominic's hand rests on my leg as if he can't bear to not touch me in some way and I know neither of us is going to get much sleep tonight.

In two days we're going to travel onto Venice, spend a few days on the canals and exploring, before heading south to Rome and then onto Pompeii and the Amalfi Coast. It's a mini tour but we'll have three weeks on our honeymoon so not so mini really and the benefit of being here is we won't be hounded, we won't be followed, we'll have some privacy.

Because despite five years passing, we're still a topic of interest for the general public to lust after. Dominic is still a big name and I've inadvertently turned myself into a minor celebrity. They call me the 'husband stealer' in the trash rags. It's amusing in a way that they're so fixed on my transgressions but no one makes comments about my mother's.

Dominic and her got divorced within months of it all coming out. Did Collin take her in? No, he didn't, turns out he was happy to shag his underling but wasn't willing to be in a real relationship which I think says a lot about him. He got fired of course. And now he pays child support for a baby neither of them wanted.

I haven't seen my mother since. Haven't spoken to her but every so often, when she's low on cash she does another circuit of the gossip rags, trying to sell her story as the woman scorned. Only everyone is getting sick of it now and besides there's only so many times you can claim to be the victim while you've got the evidence of your own misdeeds swaddled in your arms.

Do I regret what we did? No. Not for a moment. Would I change any of it? The only thing I would change perhaps is all the lies. All the deceit. When it all came out I guess it was a relief. It was over. We didn't have to hide our feelings anymore and in a way we found out who our real friends were too.

Timothy went away. He thankfully pleaded guilty, as if he could state otherwise and even now he's rotting in some prison cell. When I think back to everything he did, that thought gives me comfort.

As the evening continues Dominic gets me up to dance and I wrap my arms around his neck, stare into his face as the stars twinkle above us. It couldn't be more picturesque. It couldn't be more perfect.

"You've made me the happiest person alive." Dominic murmurs into my ear and I shake my head.

"How can you be when I am?" I say and he laughs.

"Did you see their faces, they didn't have a clue." He says nodding his head in the direction of where some of our friends are sat drinking.

I smile catching the eye of Jemma. Technically she's my agent, but we've been working together for so long and so closely, we're way beyond just professional now.

She took a punt on me when I was still the country's resident harlot. She saw something, I don't know what, but I'll be forever grateful to her for helping me achieve my other dream; of becoming a writer.

My first book came out eight months after our affair hit the press. I channelled a lot of my emotions, a lot of my energy into it as a form of escape. I think in all honesty most people bought it because of who I was. Because I was the scarlet woman who stole her mother's husband but the jokes on them because it propelled it into a bestseller.

My second book got shortlisted for the 'Women's Prize for Fiction' and, though I didn't get picked, it cemented my reputation as an actual bona fide writer. As someone to be reckoned with and not just some good time girl. It's now in the process of being made into a movie with some big Hollywood names already linked to it. Not that I'm that smug about it.

And my third? Well, if I play my cards right it should be as much of a success as the other two. So I guess I got what I wanted there too.

As the party continues around us Dominic takes my hand and quietly we escape into the dark.

I know where we're headed, what he wants, and as he kisses me every few steps along the way I'm more than a little desperate for his touch too.

We walk into what is the honeymoon suite. They've scattered rose petals all over the floor and bed. And they've lit candles too.

I glance around as Dominic starts trying to undo the countless buttons holding my dress together.

"Did you design this on purpose?" He murmurs and I laugh.

"You mean to keep you on your toes?" I say.

He grins.

"Give me a moment." I say stepping away, going into the bathroom. I've got it all planned because the underwear I've got on under this dress is absolutely not the kind I want to be wearing the first time my new husband sees me.

I slip the dress off. He's undone enough buttons for it to shimmy past my waist and then I grab the neatly hidden lingerie that's been waiting, biding its time since I put it there hours ago.

Within seconds I'm wearing a new set, white lace, bridal, with suspenders too because we've both recently discovered how much he likes me wearing them. I keep the veil on, keep my shoes on and step back into the room, back to where my husband is waiting.

DOMINIC

Epilogue

She's taking forever. Even as I'm sat, undoing my tie, kicking my shoes off, trying to get myself ready she's taking her time. Is she doing it on purpose? Deliberately teasing me?

I groan as I think of her, barely metres away, and yet it feels so far.

And then she's here and Christ, she looks incredible. She looks magnificent. She's still got the veil on, it hangs down, over her shoulders making her look more like the virginal schoolgirl I fell in love with.

She gives me an almost bashful smile.

"Let me see you properly." I say as she takes a step and I see she's wearing suspenders.

"Does your new wife meet your expectations?"

"You've always exceeded my expectations." I say back. "Every single one of them."

She takes a little intake of air. I think she's nervous, as if we haven't fucked so many times, as if we haven't seen every inch of each other's naked bodies.

"Before we do this I want you to know what my wedding gift to you is." She says stepping up right in front of me.

I wrap my arms around her, my hands kneading her ass cheeks. She's just got such incredible curves.

"I don't need any more gifts. You're all the gifts I could want." I murmur. It's true, nothing in this world could come close to her. Not a single thing.

She tilts her head. "Is that so?" She says smirking.

I narrow my eyes. "What have you bought?"

"It's not something you can buy Dominic." She says taking my hand and she places it on her belly.

My jaw drops. No way. No. It can't be. I stare up at her and she bites her lips nodding just a little.

For over a year now I've wanted to suggest we get married. I know she's wanted too, she's not exactly been quiet about it but every time the voice in my head says wait. I guess I was still afraid that, despite everything, she might change her mind but three months ago so told me she'd stopped taking her birth control. That she was ready to have a baby and that she wanted us to start our own family.

That was the final push, the final kick up the ass I needed to believe that I wasn't holding her back, that she wasn't going to resent choosing me. That she really was mine forever.

And now it's happening. It's actually happening. We're going to be parents.

"I love you so much." I say.

"I love you too." She says before grabbing my face and kissing me hard. "Now fuck your new wife like you own her."

I half growl. Fuck, this woman always knows what to say to make me lose my mind.

I pull her down, pull her on top of me. For a few minutes we do nothing but just paw at each other, grope each other, appreciate each other's bodies as we kiss and then I slip my hand into her panties.

"Crotchless?" I say as she giggles.

"You like to watch your cum dribbling out Dominic so I decided to get some underwear to help facilitate that."

I groan, plunging my fingers into her. She's so wet, so ready, and she writhes, wrapping her legs around me, riding my fingers. She's still bare, hairless. She asked once if I wanted her to get a different sort of wax but I love being able to see her flesh, see her pink lips, see the way she's flushed and swollen after I fuck her.

"You're always so ready for me." I say lowering my face to where her needy cunt is begging me to dive in.

"Ready and waiting for my husband." She gasps.

Oh I know you are. I start with small teasing licks. My tongue barely touches her and she jerks, raising her hips, increasing the contact. I let out a chuckle but I don't change what I'm doing. I'm going to lick her out, get her so close to cuming and right when she's desperate for it, I'm going to sink my cock into her and the look on her face when I do it will be incredible.

I spread her lips, pull them back with my hands. She's just such a delicacy I can't even help myself. I lick her all the way down to that perfect puckered arsehole. She shudders.

Yeah she likes that. She always has. I lick her back up and then begin to swirl. She's moaning now. Writhing more.

I plunge my tongue into her hole and she lets out a half cry, just like always. She's just so sensitive, so responsive.

And then I turn my attention back to her clit. The neediest part of her. The most demanding. In living with Eden I've learnt that all the initial passion, all the want wasn't just because we were doing something forbidden. She's actually built that way. She's got the highest sex drive I've ever known and thank god mine matches her. There's never excuses that she has a headache, hell most days she's as anxious to get my clothes off me as I am her.

And this clit of hers. This clit takes a lot of my time, a lot of my dedication, and my worship too. I roll it over my tongue, I nip at it. I've learnt how to work her fully now. She likes a little pain with her pleasure. Not a lot. Just a small hit every so often as if it increases the adrenaline, as if it heightens it all for her.

She's close, I can see it, the way she's moving, the way her cunt is flushing so red. I lift myself up, lift her too and she wraps herself around me as I sink into her.

"Dominic." She gasps.

I start thrusting then. Rocking my hips, pounding into her. She moans more, raising her body, meeting each of mine with her own. She grabs my face, she kisses me hard as my hands tighten and together we find our release.

She falls against me, leaning into my chest and I hold her so tightly.

"Happy Birthday husband." She says and I laugh.

"Happy Birthday indeed." I reply, pulling her down and we lay flat on backs with our heads turned, staring at one another.

"I can't wait to start a family with you. To have this child, to have all your children." She says.

"Oh Eden." I say, pulling her back in wrapping my arms around her. My beautiful angel, my precious wife, and now the mother of my child. I don't know how I got so lucky. I don't know what gods I honoured in another life but I will spend the rest of my days thanking them for what I have, for Eden, for the stupid mistake we made so long ago and the way this girl showed me how to live, how to love too.

Vendetta
A MAFIA ROMANCE

Take a sneak peek at 'Vendetta – A Mafia Romance'

HIM

I've been watching her all night.

Though she acts unaware I know that she knows. A girl like that isn't stupid. A girl like that isn't oblivious. The scars on her face, the scars on her body tell me that.

She walks, no glides about the space. Her body still beautiful, still wanton despite the obvious trauma.

Her hair is down. Just like always. And the curves I know she has, are hidden under the overly baggy shirt.

Preston watches her too. Just for a second before his eyes flit to the other women. The other barmaids.

In a line up, none of my men would pick Eleri. None of them would give her a second glance. They'd see the scars, they'd see the way she holds herself, no, hides herself and they'd choose one of the others. The world has brought them up to want an Instagram worthy, filter perfect image of a woman. A plastic fantastic model with perfect eyebrows, perfect lips, and a size zero body to boot.

And all the other girls try to adhere to this ridiculous ideal as if it were gospel.

But Eleri, Eleri is different. Eleri is perfect.

Two men in the corner knock over a glass and the beer splashes everywhere. Eleri is quick to respond grabbing a cloth and moving to catch the liquid before it spreads too far.

I watch as she bends over, as she gets on her knees and dabs the floor at these men's feet. One of them murmurs something and the other smirks before he looks at her properly. And then the smirk on his lips drops.

He sees the scar concealed by her hair. He sees the way her skin is marked and his face reacts in disgust.

Eleri sees it too but she doesn't say anything. She doesn't even respond. She just continues doing her job. Doing what all my other god damn staff should be doing except they're flirting right now, flirting with my men, oblivious to anything in the hopes that they might score the bigtime.

You see that's what they're all here for. That's why they work at my bar. It's not that the pays good, although it's not bad. It's not that it's glamourous. My club is where the glamour is at but this bar is where I reside most often.

And that's why they want to work here. It's because of who I am. And who my associates are and the life one of us could raise them to.

That is, everyone except Eleri, because she works here for me. Though she doesn't know it yet. She doesn't have a clue.

I've spent the last two years stalking this woman, watching from the shadows, playing her guardian angel and manipulating everything around her till I was ready to make my move.

And now I am ready.

I nod my head at the doorman and he reacts instantly signalling to everyone else to get the fuck out. It's late anyway, past last orders, but we don't play the rules here. We make our own rules.

As I lean back in my seat one of the barmaids walks up with a glass of whiskey. Neat. Just how I like it. She places it on the table in front of me and then sits down, leaning forward enough for me to get a good view of her tits beneath the curve of her tight top.

I look. It would be rude not to and then I meet her eyes. Her lips are curled. She's smiling.

"Go away." I say and her eyes widen as her face falls.

She gets up quickly. Thankfully she has enough brains not to push anything further.

Preston stares at her ass as she walks away. She's making a point of swinging her hips, as if her body could compare with the girl now hiding in the corner. Hiding in the shadows.

"You need to learn to play nice." Preston says and I laugh.

"No thanks." I say back. I don't play nice. I have no reason to.

Niceties are for fools. For weaklings. I play to win.

Preston gets up and leaves me to it. Clearly he wants to play with the barmaids and I'm more than happy for him too. He's a big boy. He can occupy his own space for a while.

My eyes flit to Eleri once more. I could wait. I could leave it another night but my skin is itching and I'm done waiting. Hell I've waited two years already. Two long, agonising years.

She makes the mistake of looking at me. Just for a moment. Her head turns enough that our eyes meet and I know then that the moment is now. She's made the decision for me. She's sealed our fate.

I beckon her to me and as she takes each slow step I see the briefest litany of emotions cascade across her face. And then the mask comes down.

My fierce beauty. My defiant snow queen becomes a statue. A perfectly unreadable stranger.

"Sit." I say quietly.

The music is still playing but it's quiet enough for her to hear me. I see her throat move, the only evidence of her nervousness now but she does what I tell her. She is obedient.

I flex my hands, unseen under the table. I'm itching to see how obedient she can be. To push her. To really test her but she's not ready and I won't rush her. At least not yet. Softly, softly, catch a beauty.

She drops her gaze, keeping her focus on the amber nectar in front of me and I take the moment to study her.

It's been a while since I've seen her face properly. It's changed so much. Evolved. The low lights bounce off her skin, illuminating the scarring as if she were a painting.

She must be wearing makeup, foundation at least to hide the redness of her skin. The thought irritates me. That she feels the need to conceal herself. To hide herself. But the way the t-shirt hides her body shows that she wants to be anonymous. Unnoticeable. A nobody.

Only my little ice queen can never be that. She will never be that.

Because I notice her. I see her. And I refuse to let her hide now.

She's breathing slowly. Calmly. I look around at the few other people nearby. Preston is busy chatting up the same girl I sent running.

But Eleri looks cool as a cucumber. As if she isn't even here. As if her she's zoned out. Her hair hangs thick over her shoulders and I want to yank on it so hard, to force her into giving some sort of reaction that I almost do it.

"Look at me." I say and she does. Again without hesitation.

Her beautiful doe eye meets mine and for a moment I think I might be lost in that look. She frowns for a moment and I take the opportunity to sip my whiskey.

She is nervous. She's skittish. Behind the façade. Behind the calm exterior this girl is like a rocket threatening to go off. I see her leg jerk for a second and I wonder if she might just flee.

"Do I scare you?" I ask her.

She nods.

I'm not surprised. Almost everyone in this city is scared of me. Or at least the smart ones are.

"What if I promise not to hurt you?" I say.

She shakes her head slightly.

"Speak. Tell me what you're thinking." I command.

"I don't believe such promises." She says.

I smirk. "Are you calling me a liar?"

"No." She replies not looking fazed. "But most men make promises they easily break."

"I am not most men."

She blinks. That's all the reaction I get. The audacity of this girl is outstanding. Perhaps that's why I want her. Why I need her.

"Can I go?" She says quietly.

I grind my teeth. On the one hand I could play nice, lull her in softly, like an injured animal, build her trust if you will but I don't think it would work and I don't have the patience for such games.

"Do you know why you work here?" I ask letting her hear the edge to my voice, looking at the vein pulsing in her neck, spiking with her adrenaline.

She nods. She works here because my bar is the only place that will employ her. None of the fancy hotels would have a girl with her face on show. None of the other bars would want her. It's here or the streets and we both know she won't choose that. Besides I've made sure she has no other options. Any other place that might hire her was told not to under no uncertain terms because I wanted her here. I needed her here. She has to be under my watch. Where I can see her. Where I can study her.

"This is my bar. I own it."

"You don't own me." She says but her face reacts. Her blood drains and I see she thinks she's made a mistake.

"Oh Eleri." I murmur and her face falls more. She didn't think I knew her name. She just assumed she was a nobody to all of us. A ghost almost. "I will own you." I say. "I will own every part of you."

She gets up, half stumbles from the stool and my men look round at the movement. I lift my hand slightly to tell them to stay where they are. I won't have them touch her. I won't have anyone touch her.

"I am not yours." She says but she's trembling. Falling apart.

I want to hold her, to feel as her body crumbles within my grasp, but I don't. I just watch as her fear takes over.

"Don't fight me Eleri." I say narrowing my eyes. But in truth I want her too. I want to see what spirit she has. I want to unleash the monster I know resides in her. That's why I chose her. That's why I stalked her.

She is no ordinary girl. The scars, the trauma attests to that.

But she's not a victim either. She's a fighter. My fighter. And I want to see how much damage she can do.

Acknowledgments

I want to express the biggest thank you to all my beautiful, sexy readers. You really are the reason that I do this, and admittedly, each book I write I want to make sexier, darker, more dramatic just for you.

Big thanks to my proof-reader extraordinaire, Caroline, who is able to polish and remove all my horrible, slightly dyslexic grammar failings, without comment or judgement.

If you're a fan and have read my previous works you'll notice this one has a distinctly different tone, it's also duel point of view. It was a first for me, but it won't be the only. In the past I mainly focused on one view but at times has felt this has skewed the reader's opinion on certain character's and with this I want to get the passion, the heat, the differing emotions of both Dominic and Eden and my first draft of this, focusing solely on Eden ended up reading like Dominic was an arsehole and an unlikable love interest – not ideal for such a plot.

This book was written and rewritten a number of times. I wanted to keep this short and steamy – veering away from the more complicated plot and character arcs that I had with the 'BlackWater Series'. My intention is to write more like this, less dark, more sexy, but I guess, like so many of my fellow writers I am bound by the whims of my own muse and no doubt she will make me eat my words more than once in the future.

I want to thank my family and friends (those who know and support me with this). Without their help and support I doubt I'd get beyond the first page. And in particular I want to thank my partner, he's nothing like the love interest I write, he's an arsehole, a sexgod, and a teddy bear, all rolled into one and how he puts up with me some days, I'm not so sure, though I won't dare pose that question to him.

If you did read and enjoy this book please leave a comment, feedback, anything that springs to mind. Your reviews really do help and I spend hours devouring them when the imposter syndrome is at it's worst.

About the Author

Ellie Sanders lives in rural Hampshire, in the U.K. with her partner and two troublesome dogs.

She has a BA Hons degree in English and American Literature with Creative Writing and enjoys spending her time, when not endlessly writing, exploring the countryside around her home.

She is best known for her spy erotica novels called 'The BlackWater Series' but has published several stand alone novels including the dark fantasy 'At The Edge of Desire'.

For updates including new books please follow her Instagram and Twitter @hotsteamywriter

Other Books by Ellie Sanders

At The Edge of Desire
Vendetta – A Mafia Romance

The BlackWater Series
Skin In The Game (Book One)
One Eye Open (Book Two)
Pound of Flesh (Book Three)

Printed in Great Britain
by Amazon